JOHN CAMERON WORKED ON STURDLEY'S COMICS BY DAY—AND LIVED THEM BY NIGHT.

The shadow was man-sized, but not quite human in form, its ears outsized and batlike. Whatever it was, it seemed at home in the murky surroundings, advancing at a steady trot on a higher, drier curve of the wall. Occasionally there was a muted scraping noise, like the sound of a fingernail—or claw—striking the concrete.

John floundered over Eddie's body, his heart pounding. The liquid was deeper, up to his ankles now, and seemed thicker. His feet pulled loose with hollow sucking sounds.

But for every step John took, the pursuer came nearer . . .

A low hissing came from ahead of him now. The creature was larger than it had seemed before, moving with a lithe bonelessness no human could emulate.

ROC

THE FUTURE IS UPON US . . .

☐ **THE ATHELING by Grace Chetwin.** In the year 2047 Earth faces its final days—and only one man's vision offers hope for survival. . . .
(451104—$5.50)

☐ **HARMONY by Marjorie Bradley Kellogg.** On a poisoned Earth where the world's great cities turn to dome technology and create their own ecospheres, where will humankind find its future? (451090—$5.50)

☐ **RAFT by Stephen Baxter.** Deep space, hard science-fiction . . . an epic tale of adventure, sacrifice and heroism. "A major new talent!" —Arthur C. Clarke. (451309—$4.99)

☐ **ARK LIBERTY by Will Bradley.** In this ecological future saga, some are building Arks to preserve as many animal species as possible. Others are seeking to destroy them. (451325—$4.99)

☐ **CHAINS OF LIGHT by Quentin Thomas.** Infinitely cloned in the datanet, he could live forever in an electronic Empire of his mind . . .
(452097—$4.99)

☐ **MARS PRIME by William C. Dietz.** On a one-way trip to colonize Mars, a killer on board marks Earth's top reporter his next victim.(452089—$4.99)

☐ **UNCHARTED STARS by Andre Norton, winner of the Science Fiction Grandmaster Award.** With a mutant at his side, a daring young trader seeks Forerrunner treasure amidst the uncharted Stars. (452321—$4.50)

☐ **FORERUNNER FORAY by Andre Norton.** Ziantha was a highly skilled sensitive stranded in a strange world where past and future mingled . . .
(451767—$4.50)

Prices slightly higher in Canada

Stan Lee's
RIFTWORLD

CROSSOVER
by Bill McCay

A ROC BOOK

ROC
Published by the Penguin Group
Penguin Books USA Inc., 375 Hudson Street,
New York, New York 10014, U.S.A.
Penguin Books Ltd, 27 Wrights Lane,
London W8 5TZ, England
Penguin Books Australia Ltd, Ringwood,
Victoria, Australia
Penguin Books Canada Ltd, 10 Alcorn Avenue,
Toronto, Ontario, Canada M4V 3B2
Penguin Books (N.Z.) Ltd, 182–190 Wairau Road,
Auckland 10, New Zealand

Penguin Books Ltd, Registered Offices:
Harmondsworth, Middlesex, England

First published by Roc, an imprint of Dutton Signet,
a division of Penguin Books USA Inc.

First Printing, September, 1993
10 9 8 7 6 5 4 3 2 1

Illustrations by Dave Gibbons
Cover by Bruce Jensen
Edited by Howard Zimmerman
Design by Dean Motter

A Byron Preiss Visual Publications, Inc. Book

INTRODUCTION

It all started innocently enough.

I was having dinner with my good friend, publisher Byron Preiss, when he casually mentioned the fact that he had produced various series of books in conjunction with such authors as Ray Bradbury and Isaac Asimov.

"How about you?" he asked. "You must have some story ideas that don't quite lend themselves to the normal Marvel comic books with which you've always been involved."

I laughed, not being quite sure the word "normal" accurately applied to either Marvel or comic books themselves. They're much too colorful and far-out. But I had to admit Byron's idea intrigued me.

Though he couldn't have known it, for the longest time I had toyed with the notion of doing a series of novels about the comic book industry—an industry that, in many ways, is just as incredible as the books it produces.

They say writers should only write about things they know. If that's the prime requirement, I've got it made!

Having personally inhabited the fantastic and fascinating comic book universe for half a century, I'm credited (or blamed, depending on your point of view) with creating, while partnered with various talented artists, *Spider-Man*, *The Incredible Hulk*, *Dr. Strange*, *The Fantastic Four*, *Daredevil* and an entire plethora of pandemonious people in skin tight suits of colorful Spandex who seem to be eternally dedicated to battling bad guys while the rest of the world goes its merry way, usually oblivious to the fact that our heroic super-dupers are saving it from certain destruction twenty-four hours a day.

At any rate, since I unquestionably possessed the proper credentials, I couldn't get Byron's suggestion out of my mind. In all my years of writing about superheroes, I always tried to make the stories take place in the real world. The Fantastic Four were possibly the first superheroes to be based in the heart of New York City instead of some fictitious "Metropolis" or "Gotham City," or wherever. The Human Torch, in his normal identity as just plain, teenage Johnny Storm, was probably the first superhero to spend his spare time polishing and tuning up his beloved Chevy Corvette rather than a clichéd "Whizbang-V8"; and certainly no superhero B.S. (Before Spider-Man) had ever lived with his elderly, eternally ailing Aunt May in a modest home in Forest Hills while attending Empire State University on a scholarship. Okay, so Empire State U. is fictitious. Hey, that was just to prove I, too, could play the game.

Reality! Though it sounds contradictory, reality is the most important element that fantasy requires. Here's a nutty example. Imagine a superhero comic book story wherein our hero (any generic superhero type) is walking down the street of Anytown and sees a ten-foot-tall, purple-faced, lizard-skinned monster with four arms, two heads, and smoke coming out of his (hers? its?) ears! Now then, years ago, before Marvel Comics pushed the medium kicking and screaming into a new "let's be realistic" phase, our typical superhero might have dramatically exclaimed, "Uh-oh! A creature from another world! I'd better destroy it before it enslaves our planet!" In fact, a reader might have been forgiven for thinking such dialogue was de rigueur for a superhero yarn. But today, chances are a hip, new-breed hero like good ol' Spider-Man would probably say, "Who's the clown in the Halloween outfit? Wonder what he's advertising?" See what I mean? Take something fantastic and give it a real-world spin!

Speaking of Spider-Man, the thing I most enjoyed doing when scripting his stories was finding unexpected ways for him to experience the same problems as you and me. Even though he has super strength and is able to crawl on walls, I got a real kick out of giving him allergy attacks during a fight, or having him plagued by an ingrown toenail, or worried about dandruff or a sudden case of acne. He was possibly the first superhero who had a problem making a living and who didn't have women swooning at his feet. Realism, remember? He was definitely my type of guy.

Incidentally, poor Spidey actually had a tough time ever seeing print. When I first pitched the idea of a wall-crawling wonder to my publisher, back in 1961, he almost chewed my head off! "People *hate* spiders!" quoth he. Then, when he heard I wanted Spidey to be a teenager at the outset: "Heroes *can't* be teenagers!

Teenagers can only be sidekicks!" If you had heard him, you'd have thought he was quoting some sacred scriptures. Finally, when I told him I also wanted our woebegone web-swinger to have lots of personal problems, he really blew a gasket. "I thought you said he was a *hero*! Heroes in comics don't have personal problems!" Lucky for me, I was too naive to be aware of those eternal truths; and the rest, if I may coin a phrase, is history.

But now, at last, Byron was proposing that I do something really different. Instead of creating comic book tales about superheroes and trying to blend them into the real world, here was my opportunity to create a series of novels about the real world itself and then add some superheroes to the mix.

The more I dwelled on it, the more the concept excited me. I kept thinking that we could use *Riftworld* to symbolically open a window between the comic book cosmos and the all-too-real universe in which we humans dwell. There was no doubt about it; the notion was a grabber—I'd create a novel, or better yet, a series of novels, based on the inspired insanity of the ever-exciting comic book business; novels in which a whole kaboodle of larger-than-life superheroes would actually appear and interact with our principal characters, all thanks to the magic of an enchanted rift between the worlds.

Then, the luckiest part of all occurred. As I agonized over the fact that, due to the pressure of an ever-increasing workload, there was no way I could write each and every story, along came Bill McCay who was eager to seize the concept and run with it. I knew that there couldn't be a better writer for such a project than the marvelous Mr. McCay, whose own "Star Trek" book had occupied a prominent spot on the N.Y. Times Best Seller list. After breathlessly beholding the wonderment awaiting you on the pages ahead, I think you'll agree that Bill actually exceeded our own high expectations.

Thus, without further ado (since we've saved all our ado for the story that follows); we enthusiastically invite you to enter a universe very much like your own, with one exception . . .

This one contains—the Riftworld!

Excelsior!

Stan Lee
Los Angeles, 1993

PRO*LOGUE*

John Cameron's foot skidded out from under him, his heel slipping on the mucky ooze trickling along the tunnel floor. He lurched, slamming into the side of the conduit with bruising force. The shoulder of his shirt tore against pitted concrete.

He shuffled forward into nearly impenetrable gloom, following the gentle downward gradient of this tunnel system. Ahead, scabrous patches of luminous muck on the walls—fungus, perhaps?—provided a wan half-light. It gave him something to aim for, at least.

John squinted down the tunnel. What was this place? He stumbled over something in the darkness, a large waterlogged obstruction.

Half-kneeling in the fetid liquid, he made out the shape of a human body.

The cold flesh had an almost pearlescent gleam, marred by gaping, bloodless gashes—talon tracks. John recognized the corpse—it was his coworker, Eddie Walcott. Eddie's staring features were frozen in an expression of horror and loathing.

Then John heard the skittering in the tunnel behind him. He turned and saw something moving, a shadow gliding against the sickly fungal glow.

The shadow was man-sized but not quite human in form, its ears outsized and batlike. Whatever it was, it seemed at home in the murky surroundings, advancing at a steady trot on a higher, drier curve of the wall. Occasionally there was a muted scraping noise, like the sound of a fingernail—or claw—striking the concrete.

John floundered over Eddie's body, his heart pounding. The liquid was deeper, up to his ankles now, and seemed thicker. His feet pulled loose with hollow sucking sounds.

But for every step John took, the pursuer came nearer.

John's nostrils filled with a raw animal stink mixed with the reek of rotted flesh. Fighting nausea, he plunged through ooze up to his knees.

The pursuer surged up out of the darkness. John got only a momentary glimpse of gray fur, red eyes, a huge paw with jagged claws extended.

He spun away, wallowing deeper into the muck where an undertow now pulled at his legs. Talons sank into the ripped sleeve of his shirt, tearing it away.

A low hissing came forward ahead of him now. The hunter leaped toward his face. The creature was larger than it had seemed before, moving with a lithe bonelessness no human could emulate. The whipcord thin body was covered with coarse gray fur—*rat* fur. A twitching muzzle thrust into John's face, sharp, rodentoid teeth showing in a humorless grin. A long, naked tail whipped around behind the creature, and those clawed paws lashed out.

John fell backward, his scream echoing off the walls, before it was drowned out by the growing roar of water. Lines of fire opened on his chest as bony claws slashed down.

He kicked out, but his feet couldn't find bottom. The current grew stronger as he choked on effluent, swirled along on a steeper gradient. Then the tube—an underground sewer, he now realized—bent in a ninety-degree downturn, and he was falling endlessly. . . .

John Cameron jerked awake, gasping for air. It had been a nightmare.

He put his hand to his pounding chest, paper crumpling under his fingers. John pulled away the comic book that had lain tented over him. On the cover, a lithe, gray-furred superhero leapt in an action pose under a stylized logo: *The Rambunctious Rodent.*

Falling back against the pillow, John stared at the comic for a moment, then flung it to the floor.

Not daring to sleep anymore this night, he lay wide-eyed and uneasy until light edged the shade at his window.

CHAPTER 1

"Put me out of my misery," Sturdley begged. "Somebody tell me this is a joke—*please*."

Gathered around the conference table was the brain trust of the Fantasy Factory—editors, marketing people, and the cream of Sturdley's art staff, veterans, and the new fan favorites. These were his creative shock troops, supposedly the best minds in the comics business. They couldn't seriously be proposing *this*.

"You're kidding, right?" Harry Sturdley took another glance at the model sheet in his hand, a series of pen-and-ink poses featuring a costumed hero with enormous muscles, a tiny head, and a huge chin. Jutting up from the character's oversized jaw was a single, razor-sharp tusk.

"Just what do you call this . . . this abortion?" Sturdley asked. "Happy Harry," as he was called in the industry, was definitely *not* happy this morning.

"I've tentatively named him the Phantom fang," Thad Westmoreland's nasal voice drawled from the far end of the table. To Sturdley's eyes, the senior editor had the appearance of a Steve Ditko villain—short and almost cadaverously thin. Westmoreland gave everyone a superior smile. Sturdley's lean face tightened into a collection of planes and angles.

"I can see where you get the name," Bob Gunnar offered, attempting to smooth things over.

Sturdley glanced toward his tall, lanky editor-in-chief. "Reminds me of the hero *you* created, Bob—the guy with the solid steel skull who rammed headfirst through walls. As I recall, you thought *Butt-head* was a swell name, too."

"Only for management," Westmoreland muttered, barely loud enough to be heard. But he was heard by the coterie of artists around him, the young turks doing the new, hot cult books: Reece Yantsey, who drew *Schizodroid*, the hero with a thousand faces; Kyle Everard, who drew *M-16, Weapon Supreme,* their character with the built-in arsenal; Zeb Grantfield, the new wonderkid. They all snickered.

Sturdley's eyes narrowed. "Yeah, the character does look funny. Downright *grotesque*."

"He's a mutant," Westmoreland explained with strained dignity. He glared at Sturdley. "And Fang is no more grotesque than Lobo or Wolverine."

"I'd say he's a lot stupider looking," Sturdley fumed. "How can the Fantasy Factory make him seem plausible? Use an origin where he gets bitten by a radioactive walrus?"

He tapped the huge, underslung jaw on one picture. "You realize, with a mug like that, he's going to catch every nose-goblin in creation. And, if I understand what you're telling me, Fang-enstein here rips out his enemies' guts with his tooth. Have you drawn that yet? It's gonna look obscene."

"That's just the kind of petty thinking we creative people keep coming up against in this company," voiced one of the younger artists. "Characters like this are the wave of the future."

"Yeah, as in wave goodbye," Sturdley said, prompting a new wave of snickering, mainly from the old warriors, Fabian Thibault and Val Innozenzio, and from Diane Jessup of production and Yvette Zelcere from marketing.

Angry color flushed Westmoreland's bony face. "Smart comments aside, Harry, the Phantom Fang is the kind of character today's more mature readers will relate to."

"You mean the teenagers who spent most of their time going to splatter movies." Sturdley tapped the picture again. "Are you saying that watching celluloid freak-shows might make them eager to buy a comic-book freak?"

Before Westmoreland could react, the door to the conference room opened. Young gofer John Cameron walked over to Sturdley and handed him a sheaf of fax pages—cumulative reports from their accountants on the previous six months' sales figures. Forcing himself not to think about John, Sturdley dismissed the kid with a wave and pointedly stared at the numbers.

"We've got something else to deal with. *Silicon Savage* is down, *The Sensational Six* is down, even *The Rambunctious Rodent* is in trouble. Sales were down last month for the sixth month in a row. That, gentlemen, is a problem. The Rodent is our flagship character. If we can't boost *his* sales, we'll all end up eating out of dumpsters."

Yvette, the Fantasy Factory's marketing director, started a now-familiar lament, which boiled down to the fact that the market was saturated. Every small company with access to a printing plant was churning out comic books. Superheroes. Funny animals. Slice-of-life stories about mass murderers. Everything from Triple-X-rated books to classic fairy tales.

"Everyone's going for a piece of the pie," Bob Gunnar said. "The problem is, the pie itself hasn't grown any. The more slices, the smaller everybody's piece becomes."

"We can't afford that," Sturdley said. "A little schmuck operation can get by with any kind of cash flow. We've got overhead to pay." His eyes took in the conference room, the large, battered table they were gathered around. He thought about the combined salary load the group represented, and the two floors of offices crammed with workers. For a moment he toyed with the idea of firing some of the high-priced talent, then rejected it. What good is lowering your overhead if you kill your ability to produce?

"We've got a nasty trend to reverse here," he finally said. "I don't want the Fantasy Factory to end up like Fawcett, or Tower, or Warren." Sturdley's face twisted as he ran through the litany of once-successful comics companies that had gone out of business. "Any suggestions on how we turn things around?"

"Thad had already pointed out one way," Bob Gunnar said, a hand going to his lantern jaw. "The competition has had some success with grittier plot-lines."

"Like what?" Sturdley demanded. "Killing off their

number-one hero? Or maybe we should turn Silicon Savage into a psycho-killer?" His lips thinned. "Dynasty Comics' idea of crime-fighting makes the Skinheads and neo-Nazis look like Boy Scouts."

"Of course, the Fantasy Factory has a much more mature approach." Thad Westmoreland's voice was corrosive as he spoke from his end of the table. "Giving Silicon Savage an eating disorder so he can't fit in his armor anymore—now that's truly appealing." His sarcasm brought another round of snickers from the younger artists clustered around him.

A tight-lipped smile came to Westmoreland's face. "Maybe the time has come to dump the neurosis-of-the-month approach, Harry. Perhaps you haven't noticed, but today's comics fans *like* seeing their heroes beat the crap out of the bad guys. Who cares about the psychological causes of anorexia?"

Sturdley felt every eye in the room look at him. He was the one who had pioneered the idea of human failings in the Fantasy Factory's heroes. That's how he was known in the industry—for that, and for getting rid of an entire crop of teenaged superhero sidekicks. "Get rid of those damn kids!" had been one of his major war cries. Of course, that had been almost thirty years ago. Back then, the Fantasy Factory had published only a handful of books. Now they had more than fifty titles a month. Sturdley had been forced to invest in enough medical texts to stock a library, digging up new frailties for an ever-growing roster of superheroes.

"Okay, maybe we've fallen into too much navel-gazing in *Silicon Savage*. But I think that's just a bad example of good policy," Sturdley said, picking his words with unusual care. "It doesn't convince me that we should follow the lead of Dynasty Comics. Their heroes are just too violent."

"Too violent?" Westmoreland asked in surprise. "This from the guy who always tells us, 'When in doubt, more hitting?'"

"There's a difference between a fistfight and a hero who eviscerates people single-toothedly," Sturdley said.

Before Westmoreland could open his mouth for an angry retort, he was cut off by a quiet voice beside him. "Maybe you just haven't had the right artist on the job."

Sturdley found himself looking into the deep-set dark eyes of Marty Burke, Westmoreland's favorite artist. Burke was also a fan favorite, hailed as a comics genius. His latest triumph was the successful revamping of Mr. Pain, a longstanding Fantasy Factory hero: thanks to an accident during brain surgery, Preston Paine had all his sensory nerves turned into reflex nerves. He could move inhumanly fast, but literally felt nothing. What could he do but become a crime-fighter? The character had coasted with middling sales for years. Then Burke took over, introducing a darker plot-line and a new character, the Echo, a beautiful, psychic corporate spy, who became Mr. Pain's lover—only to die tragically.

However, Burke hadn't spent all his time drawing comics. He had become involved in the office plotting that Sturdley had noted for more than a year now. Westmoreland had worked quietly and steadily promoting himself as the next messiah of the Fantasy Factory, who would usher in a new age of record-breaking sales after Sturdley had been forced out.

What Westmoreland didn't know—though Harry saw

it plainly—was that Marty the Genius saw *himself* in that role, the first artist to run a major comics company.

"So, Marty, you'd like a crack at *The Phantom Fang*? Kind of *ambitious* . . ." Harry paused briefly. ". . . Considering you're five months late with the eagerly awaited *Latter-day Breed* project."

Burke adjusted the jacket of his trademark black suit. "It will make sales history when it's ready," he said firmly. "And *The Phantom Fang* can do the same. If *I* create the art—and have the freedom to do it right."

The implication was obvious: the fans would buy anything with Burke's name on it. He could save the company, but he wouldn't do it for Harry Sturdley.

Harry's jaw was clenched, but there was laughter in his eyes. The fans might think Burke was a genius, but the wonderboy still hadn't figured out what made the Fantasy Factory tick. The company was held by three extended families scattered all over the country. Each shareholder had his or her own agenda, and a lot of Sturdley's job revolved around keeping them happy. Harry managed to earn autonomy for his creative team by arranging licensing deals to keep the balance sheet healthy. He knew each of the shareholders by name, marked their birthdays on his calendar, devoted much of his days to deflecting their conflicting schemes as to where the company's profits should be invested.

If Harry went, the shareholders would never allow anybody even vaguely artistic to take over the Fantasy Factory. The new boss would probably be an accountant. Burke might see himself as the savior of the company, but if he actually did force Harry out, he'd only be slicing his own throat.

"Well," Sturdley said, "neither *Breed* nor *Fang* is far enough along to help us in the short term." Sturdley swiveled his chair, turning his back on the mutineers to stare out the window at the gleaming spire of the Empire State Building. "I propose we revive a character that has a lot of known appeal."

"And what character is that?" Westmoreland wanted to know.

"The Glamazon," Sturdley responded, swinging back to face the group. "She's got a high recognition factor with the readers . . ."

His proposal was met with a collective groan from the people around the table.

"She's also had her own book three times in the last five years," Bob Gunnar pointed out. "And none of those series was a success."

Sturdley looked at his number-two man's face. Was Gunnar bailing out, too? Maybe *he* saw himself as the heir apparent.

"The Glamazon has a ready-made following." Sturdley fought to keep his voice even. "We just have to find the right presentation."

"Harry, you've tried 'em all. She's only a secondary character." Gunnar shook his head.

She's also the last character I had a direct hand in creating, Sturdley thought, still keeping a poker face. *If I had left it up to these guys, they'd have probably given her fourteen-inch industrial diamond fingernails and a taste for fresh blood.*

"The Glamazon is a known figure," Sturdley reiterated. "If we have the right story for her, the right artist, a new costume . . ."

"Oh, do I hear another of Sturdley's famous Laws

coming up?" Thad Westmoreland snipped. "Probably 'The tighter the costume, the stronger the hero?' "

Sturdley glared at the younger man. Yes, he was fond of laying down what he considered to be the laws of superhero comics. He had, after all, established the formulas that had brought the Fantasy Factory to the top of the business.

"Is fighting the only way we do business?" a lightly accented voice asked from the artists' side of the table. Elvio Vital swept black curls out of his eyes as he looked around the room. Sturdley always found an amusing contrast between the artist's wild mop of hair and his carefully trimmed mustache. Elvio had an enviable reputation as the Fantasy Factory's most dependable and most affable artist. He'd started his career in Mexico, where he'd earned fame for his ability to draw an entire comic book in a week.

Now, however, he looked weary and discouraged as he spoke. "Hey, if we don't like doing this, why don't we go do girdle ads, eh?"

The room fell silent as the younger artists stared at the tabletop, unwilling to challenge someone they all respected.

Sturdley figured the meeting needed a little distraction. He punched the intercom button on the phone at the head of the table. "Peg," he said to his secretary, "could we have some coffee, please?"

"Sure, Harry," Peg said. "I'll send somebody in."

Sturdley clicked off the intercom. It would probably be best if Peg didn't bring the coffee herself. She was almost the perfect Wally Wood woman—in illustration terms, "five heads high" and extremely curvy. Male eyes wandered and egos preened in front of his redheaded assistant. Every artist in the Fantasy Factory tried his luck with her. Sturdley had shamelessly moved her desk right outside his office as a lure for past-deadline illustrators. They came like lemmings to talk to her, right into bawling-out range.

The only artist he hadn't seen there was Marty Burke. Either the Genius had the sense to stay away while he was late, or perhaps he felt his status in the organization meant Peg should come to *him*.

Harry looked at the buzz of side-conversations going on during the impromptu break. Thad Westmoreland huddled with Burke and their coterie of younger artists. Elvio Vital doodled on his notepad. Bob Gunnar leaned over to mutter, "Harry, I wish you'd let me know when you're going to drop these bombshells."

Sturdley shrugged. "Sorry, Bob, but it was a spur-of-the-moment kind of thing. I had to do something to counter the insurrection."

Gunnar directed a worried gaze at Burke. "We can't afford to lose him right now," the editor-in-chief said.

"If this keeps up, we can't afford to keep him," Sturdley said. "These are supposed to be status meetings, not civil wars."

The door opened, and when Harry saw it was John Cameron who stood with the tray, he wished he'd asked Peg to bring the coffee herself.

Sturdley couldn't explain his problem with Cameron. There was just something about the kid that made his teeth itch. He'd seen lots of goofier-looking kids among the hundreds who'd allowed themselves to be exploited as office gofers for a chance to get behind the scenes of a comics company. Usually, they had divided into two types: tall and skinny, and short and fat. He glanced down the table at Burke. When he'd joined as a gofer, he had been of the short and fat type. As his fame grew, his waistline had shrunk. And his royalties had allowed him to hire expensive tailoring to conceal his stocky form.

John Cameron, however, broke the gofer mold. He was tall and fat. Or *was* he fat? Looking at the stocky form in the doorway, Sturdley realized he couldn't be sure. Cameron obviously had a big, deep chest. But between the layers of sweatshirts and the shapeless sweater he wore, the kid could be packing muscle, fat, or the world's biggest moneybelt.

He wasn't the ugliest kid who'd ever worked for the Fantasy Factory. Sandy-brown tousled hair topped a square, blocky face, with the right number of eyes and ears. Focusing on the figure with the tray, Sturdley now realized what bothered him: John Cameron's face looked oddly *unfinished*, like a rough Jack Kirby pencil sketch. A good inker might even make him look handsome. But an inker isn't what the kid needed. A psychiatrist, maybe.

What really disturbed Sturdley about the kid was the typical look on John Cameron's face as he stood frozen in the doorway. It was that vacant, nobody-lives-here expression he usually wore.

"Well?" Thad Westmoreland needled, "are you going to stand there until the coffee's cold, or will you get around to serving it?"

The vacuous look vanished as John Cameron's expression snapped into focus. "Sorry," the kid said, rushing toward the table. Was it a trick of the light, or did Cameron's eyes, which had seemed colorless in the doorway, suddenly gleam a bright blue?

The kid worked his way around the table, silently, with an almost absurd look of hero-worship on his face. *You'd think he'd been called to serve coffee at Valhalla,* Sturdley thought ironically.

Then he noticed another weird thing. Without asking or being told, the kid was depositing different kinds of coffee in front of each member of the conference. The coffee in Burke's cup was extra light, while Westmoreland's brew was extra dark.

John Cameron paused behind Sturdley, selected a cup, and placed it down. Happy Harry looked at it for a second, then tasted: coffee, black, three squares.

How does he do that? Sturdley wondered. *One second you're not sure he's even connected to this planet. The next, he handles a coffee order for more than a dozen people perfectly, without even asking.* A slight shudder ran down Sturdley's back. *It must have been Peg. She probably arranged the tray, wound the kid up, and sent him in.*

Sturdley took another sip of the coffee, then set his cup down. The distraction had done its work, dissipating the tension in the air. "Okay, let's get back on the job. We need something to goose sales in the short term. There are all those stockholders out there to keep happy."

Dead silence met him from the table.

Then Kyle Everard, one of the younger artists near Burke, spoke up. "Why not devote a book to one of our more popular *Villains*? Then we wouldn't have to worry about good and evil, all this neurosis crap, plots, or anything. The bad guys can just rock and roll, whaling away on each other."

Harry Sturdley lost it. "What the hell do you think

comics are about?" he shouted, leaping from his chair. "The whole basis is *good* versus evil. We aren't in the business of glorifying villains. We offer *heroes* to catch the fans' imaginations. At least, that's what we're *supposed* to do."

He directed a searing glance around the table, aiming his words at Burke's coterie. "It's too damn bad we don't have bona fide superheroes in real life. Then we could take our stories from the newspapers, and get rid of some of the deadwood around here."

"You mean, you want a Crossover?"

Harry Sturdley turned in surprise at the new voice. It was John Cameron, who was hovering by the door.

"A crossover? Yeah, kid," Sturdley's voice was crushingly sarcastic. "Maybe you can cross us over some super-powered mutants to clean up this city. Nice-looking types whom no one knows about, with interesting powers and a deep desire to become Fantasy Factory characters. Preferably, they should live in New York and provide their own skintight costumes."

Sturdley began to turn away as John Cameron rushed out the door, glancing back with an eager smile, as if he'd just been given an important job. *It must be a trick of the fluorescent lights out in the hallway,* Sturdley thought. *Now the kid's eyes seem so dark, they look almost purple.*

"A crossover isn't such a bad idea, Harry." Bob Gunnar spoke up as the door closed. "We haven't done one in a while. Linking together several series with a crossover plot gave us huge sales boosts in the seventies."

"Yeah," Westmoreland grumbled, "until the fans finally rebelled against having to buy six books at a time to follow the storyline."

"What's going to link them?" Elvio Vital asked.

Bob Gunnar glanced at his boss. "How about the Glamazon? Harry's right when he says she's got a following."

Harry Sturdley carefully retained his poker face. Okay! Gunnar was back on his team.

"I've even got the plot twist," Harry said to the others. "We set her up as the antagonist for our best heroes. Ol' Glamazon is pretty tough. We can face her off against our heavy hitters." He allowed himself a grin, although he didn't aim it at Burke, Westmoreland, and their followers. "We can have *lots* of hitting."

"What are we going to present about the Glamazon that nobody's seen before?" Burke sneered. "With that last costume change, she showed off just about everything she's got." Behind the sarcasm was a direct challenge to Sturdley's leadership. Burke continued putting down Harry's most recent brainchild. "Maybe if we have a character who beats her, humiliates her, drags her naked through the mud—"

"Why don't you just kill her and be done with it?" Harry burst out. A look of wonder passed over his face. "Yeah—kill her. We'll do a limited crossover series— present *The Death of the Glamazon* in a special shrink-wrapped collectors' edition, then flash back on how it happened. We can use the *Rambunctious Rodent, The Sensational Six,* and Glamazon's arch-rival, Madam Vile. Could you pull that off, Marty?"

Burke sputtered, caught totally off-guard. "Well, of course. I mean, if anyone can, I . . . but there's a lot of work still to be done on *Latter-Day Breed*."

"Hey, I can give it a shot, if Burke's too busy," Zeb Grantfield offered.

The look Burke shot at the young artist was downright corrosive. Stabbed in the back, by someone who was supposed to be in his hip pocket.

"No, no, no," Burke said, sounding almost as petulant as the Lump. "It's my idea. I'll give it a go."

Sturdley allowed a small smile to tug at his lips. "Okay. Let's work it out."

Revitalized, Sturdley plunged into the planning. Running with a new storyline in several books meant juggling the production schedule. But the editors responded with growing enthusiasm as they realized the possibilities. For one thing, they could get Silicon Savage off his anorexic butt and back into his armor.

Harry was pleased. This would silence the whispers that Happy Harry Sturdley was past his prime. He glanced down the table at the younger artists still clustered around Marty Burke. Maybe he could drive a wedge in there, offer some of the young guys a chance to redesign the Glamazon's look. She needed a new costume . . . something tighter. . . .

The success of the meeting carried Sturdley through to the afternoon. At least for the time being, he'd stopped Burke and his mutineers. Time was on Sturdley's side, and he'd gained a lot of time with this new crossover. Who'd have ever thought John Cameron would make a useful suggestion?

He returned to his office to find Peg Faber at her desk with a handful of pink "While You Were Out" messages.

"You got a call from Cousin Louie," she said.

Sturdley sighed. Sixty years ago, the Fantasy Factory had been founded by three partners: Louis Fanchik, Louis Fanciullo, and Lawrence O'Fanahan. In those innocent days, they'd been known as the three Fan-boys. Today, proliferating families had created all too many Cousin Louies and Cousin Larries, each with their shares of Fantasy Factory stock. "Which Cousin Louie?" he asked.

"Sell-out-to-a-big-corporation-now Cousin Louie," Peg promptly answered.

Sturdley sighed louder. That actually was one of his *wife's* cousins. "I'll take care of it later—" he began. Then the world seemed to dim around him. Reality took a sudden, sickening *twist*. The floor disappeared from under his feet, threatening him with a fall into infinite emptiness.

Gasping, Sturdley clutched at the edge of Peg's desk. Slowly, the world lurched back to normal, and he felt solid floor beneath his feet again.

"Harry, are you all right?"

Sturdley focused on two wide gray eyes looking at him in concern. "I'm fine now," he assured Peg. As soon as he could trust himself to move, he walked slowly to his office door.

"Peg," he said quietly, "I'm going to be busy in here for a while."

Peg Faber's mass of red curls bobbed as she turned to face her boss. "Harry, I think I should call a doctor."

"No, really—I'm okay. Hold my calls. Including Myra. If she does ring in, just tell her I'm tied up in meetings. I'll see her at home around seven."

He shut the door and tottered for his desk.

Sturdley dropped into the leather executive chair he'd inherited when the Fantasy Factory took over this floor from a bankrupt publishing house. He'd gotten the publisher's office, and the publisher's out-of-work assistant—Peg. Now the wood-paneled chamber was decorated with drawings of Fantasy Factory characters, signed by the artists who had drawn them, and by Sturdley, who'd created them. Harry paid no attention to the sketches, nor did he look at the papers piled on the big, baroque desk. These were the new licensing revenue figures, a sop to the stockholders. And there were details on the chances for getting a *Sensational Six* show onto that new cable network—a marginal prospect at best.

Sturdley closed his eyes and let out a long breath, more like a groan than a sigh. What had happened to him at Peg's desk? Was it just a reaction from the hostilities at the staff meeting? He wasn't getting any younger. Fifty had passed a bunch of birthdays ago. That's why the politicking had begun—the young turks smelled blood and were jockeying for position, but he couldn't let that happen. The Burkes and Westmorelands would screw everything up—everything the shareholders didn't destroy.

So what *had* happened? A mild heart attack? A stroke? He'd have to talk it over with Myra, maybe call a doctor. . . .

Sturdley stayed slumped back in his office chair, leaving a few more gray hairs on the headrest. He opened his eyes and swung the chair to face the north window of his corner office. The Fantasy Factory was based in an old office building in Manhattan's upper Twenties, technically south of the midtown high-rise district.

But thanks to a quirk of sightlines, Harry's office, like the conference room, had a fairly decent view. Beyond the wooden water towers atop nearby buildings,

Harry found never-ending comfort in admiring the magnificent art deco spire of the Empire State Building.

Ruefully, Harry glanced toward the phone. Maybe Peg was right. He should call a doctor.

He turned his chair toward the desk—then whipped it back to the window so fast the chair's bearings screeched.

Harry Sturdley squinted, not sure if he believed his eyes. There seemed to be a figure climbing the side of the 104-story building—a figure subtly out of scale with the rest of the picture. As the climber paused, clinging to a window ledge, Harry realized that he had to be nearly two stories tall. Okay. The Empire State was a pre-central-air-conditioning building with high ceilings—that meant the climber had to be at least twenty feet tall.

Sturdley shook his head. *Am I hallucinating?*

Then Happy Harry peered harder. "Well, he's not hairy enough to be King Kong," he finally muttered. "What the hell is going on?"

CHAPTER 2

Standing on the southwestern corner of Thirty-fourth Street and Fifth Avenue, Robert glared up at the figure climbing the side of New York's most famous building. A frown twisted his handsome, regular features as he tossed his head, flinging back a mane of golden hair. His hands bunched into fists, outlining cords of muscle on his bare arms and chest. *Wherever this place is,* he though, *it's warmer than home.* Not that he minded. His kind only wore brief clouts around their loins, no matter what the weather. Mental auras protected them from the worst excesses of Mother Nature.

Now, standing in this alien place with its surprisingly strong noonday sunshine, Robert had other things on his mind. It was bad enough being suddenly thrust into a strange new world, but he had the bad luck to be thrust here with a total moron for company.

Moments before, Robert had knelt behind a thicket in the Master's woods, listening to someone thrashing noisily through the underbrush. Then he'd seen Maurice and realized he faced another fugitive, not the hunters.

He had intended to let the wastrel pass, to draw any pursuit, when suddenly his world had fallen away with a sickening *twist*. And then they were here.

Instead of leaf mold, the ground beneath him was harder than the toughest packed earth. Robert had risen to his feet to find a wild-eyed Maurice facing him. At first, Robert thought they were in some sort of stone valley. Then he realized the valley walls were too steep, broken too regularly—and had numerous rectangular openings with Lesser Ones peering out. These stone canyons had been *built*.

His immaterial senses screamed with the presence of thousands upon thousands of Lessers. They were crammed inside the stone edifices; they filled the areas around the towers; they were even inside the beetle-like creatures coursing along the floor of this artificial valley. No, the moving things were also constructions, he now realized, *operated* by the Lessers inside.

Maurice's response had been typically brainless. First he'd bleated, "Where are we?"

Then, terrified by the same sensations that threatened Robert's equilibrium, Maurice had begun scaling one of the larger constructions, using the windows as finger- and toe-holds.

Robert did not hide the look of disgust he sent upward at his companion. Climb as Maurice might, he wasn't going to find a path home.

That was behind them now. And, in Robert's opinion, it was a far better thing. At home, he had no hope for advancement. But here . . .

The twenty-two-foot-tall Robert looked around at the huge structures on all sides. He could tell now that they had all been built by Lessers. That led to the conclusion that none of his kind were here, wherever *here* might be. His people would never allow such a concentration of Lessers. Nor would they permit these constructions that towered over him.

Robert found the stone piles oppressive. How must these smaller beings feel?

A slow smile passed over his lips. Of course, the structures probably served a deeply felt need for the Lessers. They needed something—or someone—looming over them.

With that thought, he turned his attention to the crowd of Lessers clustered around his feet. None of them stood higher than his knees. And it was obvious they'd never seen one of his kind. He sensed the fear in some of their minds, but it was outweighed by avid curiosity.

"He's like a living statue." Robert caught the snatch of thought. "Like a Greek god."

Robert had no notion what "Greek" meant. But he recognized the word "god."

Good. They would learn.

As Cheech Tamino made his way through the mass of people, he thought of something he'd seen in a book of cartoons he'd stolen a year or two ago. The sketch showed two businessmen passing a gaggle of bystanders who blocked their view while staring at the spectacle of another tycoon being attacked by an octopus emerging from a manhole. The tag line was, "It doesn't take much to collect a crowd in New York."

Watching the gaping multitude around him, Tamino happily admitted to himself that the cartoonist had it right. Every eye in the crowd was glued to one or the other of the two big guys who'd appeared from no-where.

Cheech had stopped looking as soon as he realized everyone else was distracted. This was the kind of break he needed for his new business venture—purse-snatching.

The woman he'd targeted was leaning way back, her mouth open almost as wide as the top of the satchel bag dangling from her shoulder. Perfect!

Cheech moved forward, zig-zagging through the throng. He lunged between two business-suit types, pushed up to the woman, and seized hold of one of the straps on the bag.

The woman was almost flung to the ground before the strap broke. Cheech took off, bursting between the two suits again. By the time they got their eyes down to ground level, he had disappeared into the crowd. Behind him, the woman was letting off a scream like an air-raid siren.

Let her yell, Cheech thought. *Better than trying to run after me.*

Robert sensed the crime as merely the slightest disturbance, nearly lost in the crowd around him. But the commotion rippled outward, enlarging, until he was able to zero in on its center—strong emotions of shock, anger, and twisted triumph. A crime . . . a theft. And the thief was making his escape, barely hindered by the distracted multitude.

Robert took a step forward, heedless as the crowd shrank back. In any event, he was used to that response from Lessers. He pressed on, a clear path opening through the crowd as he advanced on the wiry thief.

The bunching of people now impeded the thief, who, according to Robert's mental probe, rejoiced in the name of Cheech. Even with an open field, however, Cheech couldn't have outrun him.

Robert now looked down on the thief. Cheech glanced over his shoulder and froze, his eyes going wide with disbelief and dread. The petty bandit redoubled his efforts to get away.

He got nowhere, though. Robert was upon him, reaching down with a hand that, to Cheech's scale, was a foot wide. At first, Robert tried to catch the fleeing felon by his shirt. He knew from grim experience that a hasty grab at a Lesser could have unfortunate results for the grabee.

Knockwurst-like fingers grabbed the back of Cheech's polo shirt. His response was immediate—he shucked the garment off.

Scowling, Robert dropped the shirt and lunged to corral Cheech. The purse-snatcher tried to dive under the oncoming obstruction, only to have Robert's other hand pounce on his lower leg.

This time, Robert was less concerned with the careful approach. He maintained a firm hold on Cheech's leg as he rose, dangling the thief at arm's length.

Cheech squawked as he swung upside-down, his eyes glued to the cold, hard pavement a good dozen feet below. His muscles clenched in fear, one arm still clutching the stolen satchel to his chest.

"H-hey!" Cheech gabbled, suddenly finding his voice. "Get off me!"

"I should think that you are on *me*," Robert responded in the thief's tongue—plucked from his mind—his voice a low, threatening rumble.

"Yo, man, you can't drop me!" the thief yelled. "I got rights! I'm protected by the law!"

"Are you protected against gravity?" Robert inquired coldly.

He spotted several men dressed in identical uniforms working their way through the crowd. From his sense of the blue-clad figures, and reading the responses of the multitude, Robert realized they were some sort of authorities—thief-takers.

Robert also sensed that the newcomers carried weapons. If he understood their minds correctly, they seemed to consider firing some sort of small projectiles at him.

One of the blue-clad arrivals—a young one, Robert saw in his mind—had already unsheathed his weapon. Now he fired. Robert heard the surprisingly loud report. An instant later, he felt an impact in the aura that surrounded his body. It was strong enough to surprise Robert, staggering him slightly and eliciting new yelps of terror from his prisoner.

But the projectile did not penetrate.

The officers—as he now read their titles in the minds of the crowd—stared for a second, somewhat disconcerted to find Robert unhurt. Then one of them, apparently depending on a familiar formula, cried, "Police! Freeze!"

Robert looked down on the advancing blue-clad ring. "This man is the lawbreaker," he said, depositing Cheech Tamino softly on the ground. "He is a thief. The bag in his arms belongs to this woman." He pointed unerringly through the crowd to the near-hysterical victim.

Cheech Tamino tried his best. "What bag?" he de

manded unsteadily, now letting his prize fall to the ground. "I never saw that thing before! He musta planted it on me!"

"While you were hanging upside down from his hand?" one of the policemen inquired as he produced a pair of handcuffs. He looked up at the figure poised over them and shouted, "I guess we owe you some thanks, big guy."

"I can hear you perfectly well, Officer. And my name is Robert."

"Robert what?"

The giant's handsome features twisted in puzzlement. "Just *Robert*."

"Okay then, uh, Robert. We have to ask you and your buddy up on the building for a favor." The officer glanced up toward Maurice, who had stopped at the third setback on the Empire State Building and was now heading back down. "Look, this is a very busy area of the city, and your being here is tying everything up."

The crowd had indeed grown to strangling proportions, and the stream of moving vehicles had stopped like clotted blood.

"Where can we go?" he asked.

"We should take 'em downtown," one of the other officers said.

"On what charge?"

"Obstructing traffic."

"They'll only do that worse if we take 'em down to Centre Street." An older man frowned in thought. "How about Central Park?"

He took off his hat, running a hand through grizzled gray hair. "Look," the officer said to the giant figure, "there's a place north of here. A park."

Robert frowned, getting the impression of greenery. "An open space?"

"Yeah. Trees, grass, a place away from traffic. I think that's where you should go. It's maybe a mile and a half away—" The officer stopped, frowning. "You know how far that is?"

"I can understand."

"Good. Would you and your friend go up there? It would help clear up this traffic jam . . . we'd really appreciate it."

"You're just going to let them walk away?" another officer demanded.

"You think we'll have a problem finding them again?" the older man asked. "Looks to me like they'd be hard to miss."

Maurice had now descended to ground level, the crowd shifting again as he made his way carefully over to Robert.

"What's going on?" Maurice sent the frantic thought to Robert, turning brown spaniel eyes up to meet those of his companion in adversity. Maurice was a good foot shorter than Robert, though by local measure he was over twenty feet tall. His dark hair was wind-tousled, and his delicate but slightly flabby features were damp with sweat. "I looked and Searched . . ."

Robert opened his mind to the results of Maurice's mental scan. Uncounted numbers of Lessers surrounded them. But, as Robert had suspected, there were none like him and Maurice to be found.

"We're lost . . . alone." Maurice was almost gibbering with fear.

Robert thrust his will at his companion. "If you need

to show fear, show it to me mind-to-mind, where the Lesser's can't see."

Maurice had lost all control of his mind-shields. His thoughts poured out almost incoherently. "Trapped among Lessers. Can't go home."

"And were you all that happy in the former home which you now feel so passionate about?" Robert brutally shot back. "You had no choice but to leave the Master's place."

"And you as well," Maurice sulkily responded.

"Yes," Robert agreed, a glint of menace in his thought. "We have nothing to return to. But we have opportunities *here*. While you were above, did you observe my little adventure?"

"I caught the disturbance. A thief—and some kind of attack?" Maurice now sent an apprehensive glance toward the authorities in blue.

"The elder one has taken the thief and directed us to a place more like home." Maurice shifted in his buskins. "At least, less hard underfoot."

"Like home?" The look on Maurice's face was almost pathetic.

"No. No more of us are here. Do you realize what that means?"

Maurice's big brown eyes remained uncomprehending.

"It's the chance of a lifetime for a landless pair like ourselves. These people need us, Maurice. They fear crime. They need the order we can give them."

At last, the possibilities began to dawn on the shorter giant.

Robert took his companion by the arm and started

north. Perhaps Maurice could think better with grass under his feet.

"Come on," Robert said, walking carefully so as not to trample any of his newfound charges. "We have much to discuss."

He glanced around the cityscape. "And to plan."

CHAPTER 3

Robert was feeling footsore and frustrated by the time he and Maurice reached the stretch of parkland the officer had told them about. The blond giant was still unused to the hardness of the ground under his buskins. He was also furious at constantly breaking his natural stride to avoid stepping on innumerable Lessers who kept crowding in to stare at him.

They do not know to keep their proper distance, he thought angrily. Then: *How could they? These Lessers have never seen ones like us before.*

The man dashed madly away as a huge foot nearly crushed him. For a second, he was pressed against a building wall as the crowd following the giant swept up the avenue. Then, trailing behind the mob, his friends came up, holding up his suit jacket and briefcase. "Okay, Bob, we each owe you a martini," one told him.

"That's just as well," he answered, "because the ones I had before are suddenly all gone."

"I guess nearly getting stomped by a giant has a sobering effect," the other joked.

"Tell you one thing," Bob said, "you're more full of hot air than they are. The soles on those boot-things the blond guy is wearing are pretty worn. That puts a pin in your balloon theory."

Two maintenance men standing in the building's doorway avidly eavesdropped on the conversation. "See, amigo, I was right," said the one with "Ralph" embroidered on his green coveralls. "Robots," he said in a portentous voice. "Five will get you ten it's robots."

They all stared after the giant pair moving steadily northward. "I still don't get it," Bob muttered. "If it's a movie, where are the cameras? When Schwarzenegger shot in Times Square, there were weeks of warning. With a thing this size, wouldn't it be easier just to super it in?"

From Thirty-fourth Street on north, police radios blared into life, calling cops to Fifth Avenue. Patrolman Dennis O'Shea was enjoying the first bite of his meal break when the call came over his walkie-talkie.

"Nrmmmmmmmph!" he said, pointing at his full mouth. His rookie partner, a petite black woman with a Jamaican accent, took the call.

"Crowd control?" he echoed when the mouthful of hamburger was finally swallowed. "We lose our meal for this?" He stared moodily at the rest of the burger platter in front of him.

Vonnie Bates, his young partner, just shrugged. "Must be some sort of unexpected demonstration," she said in her lilting voice.

"Honey, you just hope it don't turn into a riot,"

O'Shea said grimly. "I don't wanna be stuck covering your ass as well as mine." He set his cap on his head, hefted his nightstick, and led the way out of the restaurant.

The cross-street they were on was north of the approaching crowd. The officers reached Fifth Avenue in time to get a perfect view of the advancing giants.

"Jesus, Mary, and Joseph," Dennis O'Shea burst out, awestruck. "They'll have to change the old saying now."

"What old saying?" Vonnie Bates wanted to know.

" 'Two's company, three's a crowd.' " The patrolman pointed to the giants. "At their size, *two's* a crowd."

Outside the mayor's office, a cluster of city officials spoke unhappily among themselves.

"He's got to know," the police commissioner said. "Sooner or later, the press will be asking him questions. We can't let him look like the dope of all time."

"We don't want to move too hastily," a deputy mayor warned.

"Maybe we can declare a state of emergency," the deputy mayor's assistant suggested.

That led to a happy hum of consideration. Emergencies usually meant an influx of state and federal funds.

The police commissioner poured cold water on that, however. "The giants haven't done anything yet," he pointed out. "They've just walked uptown, tying up traffic."

"Which has been a severe hardship to many of my constituents," a councilman broke in. "Stores haven't been able to get deliveries. People have been calling my office about being trapped in parking lots, unable to get out because of the traffic volume. It's worse"—he paused for a second, trying to come up with a suitable comparison—"it's worse than what happens around Rockefeller Center at Christmastime!"

The police commissioner sighed. "We usually don't declare the giant Christmas tree a cause of emergency, so I don't think we can declare one because of giants— not till they do something. They're not like a blizzard or a hurricane."

"Or an earthquake," added the deputy mayor's assistant, earning glares from everyone.

"Well, I'm going to suggest a fact-finding panel," the councilman suggested. "Maybe we should call the mayor of Tokyo. They always have problems with giant monsters, don't they?"

Leslie Ann Nasotrudere gave her cameraman a furious glare. "You know, *First News* isn't the only game in the world," she said. An ugly scowl marred the near-Barbie-Doll prettiness of her facial features.

"Sure," scoffed Angie, her heavyset cameraman. "There's the network. You're always telling them you've got the perfect mug and chest for a national news job. But did you get the position on *Thirty-six Hours*? Nooooo." He gave her a dirty look. "And do you want to know why? It's because everybody knows what a poisonous bitch you are."

"I am not!" she flared back. "I'm a hard-hitting reporter, with awards to prove it."

"I think you've been reading your promos so long, you're beginning to believe them."

The argument was interrupted by the bleating of the cellular phone. Leslie Ann picked up the receiver. "Got something for us?" She frowned. "Police band messages warning of an out-of-control crowd? Big? Charlie, this better not be some bullshit demonstration. I've gotten stuck with three of them this week."

She turned to the driver of the van. "Fifth and Fifty-ninth."

As the van went into a screeching turn, Angie gave the news star a sour look. "And if it is just another demonstration?"

"I'll come up with an angle," Nasotrudere said airily. "News is what you make of it."

Sixth Avenue and Fifty-ninth was a perfect choke-point for the homeless window-washers. Traffic ground to a near-standstill as cars approached Central Park. Most of them turned onto heavily-trafficked Fifty-ninth Street, a process that usually took a waiting time of two lights, minimum. The drivers were now stuck for the duration, sitting ducks for the guys with the squeegees and dirty rags, smearing their windows for a small "contribution."

The homeless man stepped back in disgust as the driver of the Cadillac started up his wipers. "Cheap mother," he muttered. "If'n he can afford a car like that, he should be able to gimme somethin'."

A flurry of movement over by Fifth Avenue caught his eye. He stared as a pair of twenty-foot-tall men strode past the Plaza Hotel and into the park. The homeless man was so dumbfounded, he didn't notice the light had changed. Dodging the Cadillac that nearly clipped him, it's wipers still running, he shouted a query to heaven and anyone else on the street. "What kinda prio'ties we got in this here country? They can make guys that tall and can't put a roof over my head?"

Peg Faber shuffled papers on her desk, trying to look busy but just going through the motions. She was uncomfortably aware of the heavily varnished office door closed behind her. Harry Sturdley was famous for his open-door policy. Often he'd appear in the doorway to chat with people passing by, occasionally asking in some of the office gofers to solicit their opinions on new art or plot twists. Sometimes he'd tell her, "No calls." But his door was *never* shut.

What if Harry were really sick in there? His face had been so gray as he'd walked away from her desk. In the ten months since he'd rescued her from the wreck of the floundering publishers who had occupied these offices, Peg had moved from gratitude to respect for her boss. Oh, he was a perfect *crazy genius* type, erratic and sometimes demanding. But she'd been through that before, and Harry Sturdley had the advantage of being likable as well.

Peg also had to admit a selfish worry. She'd been around long enough to know that if Sturdley left the Fantasy Factory, the company would go down the drain, and with it, her job.

Working with Harry Sturdley had been weird, but at least she was working on the fringes of publishing. The assistant's position would tide her over until a real editorial job came along. Comic books were *not* literature. But surprisingly, she found herself doing more editorial work than she had at the failed press. And where else would she get to act as a one-person shareholder-relations department?

She shuddered at the thought of Thad Westmoreland trying to run things. He'd never be able to control the artists—a notoriously horny lot, coming around her desk, showing how they'd drawn her into their books. As far as she could see, the only feature they got right was her red hair. These tall, skinny, stretched-out and over-developed females bore little resemblance to her.

Marty Burke, however, had never drawn Peg. He hardly even talked to her. But Peg could feel his eyes on her sometimes. It was as if he expected to find her on his drawing board someday, not in ink, but in the flesh—flopped on her back.

The door to the publisher's office abruptly burst open, and an animated Harry Sturdley leaned out. "Hey, Peg! You've got a radio stashed in your desk, don't you?"

She nodded.

"Turn on one of those all-news stations."

Peg looked a little surprised. "Are you looking for anything in particular?"

Sturdley gave her a peculiar smile. "Oh, I think you'll know it when you hear it."

Digging the little portable out of her desk drawer, Peg flicked it on. The sound came up right in the middle of the traffic report. "—a traffic advisory to stay away from Midtown, especially Fifth and Thirty-fourth, because of police activity. Believe it or not, Jim, Call-In Central has been flooded with reports of a pair of twenty-foot giants on the street there."

Peg spun her chair around to face the now-empty doorway. "Only in New York," she muttered.

Harry Sturdley turned from his northern window as Peg came in. "What's the story on this giant guy?"

"There are two of them, and they're blocking traffic."

Sturdley laughed. "I could have guessed that, after

seeing one of them climbing up the Empire State Building."

Peg glanced toward the window. "You saw him climbing?"

"A regular King Kong. Reminded me of a series we did back in '63, in the old *Unlikely Tales*. Called the character Bigman. The gimmick was that in each issue, he kept getting bigger. In the end, he got *too* big and died."

Sturdley came out of his reverie to find Peg peering out the window, checking the sightline to the Empire State. "Pantagruel," the young woman murmured.

"Who?"

Peg turned around. "You now, Gargantua and Pantagruel. I read translations from Rabelais' giant tales in college. Pantagruel was my favorite giant. He was always out to get a drink." She gave Sturdley a crooked grin. "Sort of like most of my college friends."

"Gargantua, huh? Good name for a character. Maybe we can use it. Is this Rabelais guy still around?"

Peg opened her mouth, then abruptly closed it. Yes, this definitely wasn't real publishing. "Rabelais died in 1553."

Sturdley shrugged. "No copyright problems, then. Gargantua and . . . no, Pantagruel won't work. Too hard to pronounce. The fans won't go for it. We need something else. Maybe a female. They loved the old fifty-foot women movies. A giant female superhero . . . what kind of name for her, though? Giant, titan . . . there it is: Titania. Tight costume, lots of cleavage . . ."

"Titania was the queen of the fairies," Peg spoke up. "Shakespeare used her in *A Midsummer Night's Dream*."

"That's not a good image," Sturdley said with a frown. "Let's drop that for the time being. This whole giant thing looks like a publicity stunt to me, and that points to the competition. The people at Dynasty Comics don't care what they do to their universe, as long as they can get free advertising. Look at what they did to their best-known hero—Zenith, the Man of Molybdenum. They killed him off and then brought him back four months later."

Still frowning, he stared out the window. "The news only talked about the traffic jam side of things? No mention of where these guys came from? That's not like Decrepit. They'd have a big banner with their corporate logo over these guys. But the one I saw climbing looked like he was wearing a diaper. What kind of superhero is that? Everybody knows—"

Peg sighed, quoting sacred writ: "The tighter the uniform, the stronger the hero."

"You laugh, but it's true," Sturdley told her. "Now go out and get some more info on these guys."

Peg returned to her desk and the radio:

"This is really incredible, Jim. The shorter of the two giants has to be around twenty feet tall, and the other is a good foot taller. They're both prime physical specimens, deeply tanned, and wearing—well, I don't know what to call it. Something between a loincloth and swaddling clothes, I guess."

Peg felt Harry Sturdley's presence in the doorway behind her chair. "Well? Anything more?"

"They're giving a blow-by-blow of the giants' progress uptown," she reported. "But there's no mention of where these guys come from—or who's behind them."

Harry Sturdley came out and sat on the edge of Peg's

desk, looking baffled. "That doesn't sound like a publicity stunt. If this were a shill for a movie or TV show, we'd have heard of it already. The producers would be trying to sell us a license to do a comic of it."

"Something else doesn't make sense," Peg said suddenly. "One of my professors in college gave a course on human limits. According to him, no accurately measured human has been taller than nine feet. He claimed it was biologically impossible for us ever to grow more than twelve feet tall and still stand upright. So how could these guys actually be twenty feet tall? Unless maybe the newspeople are exaggerating."

Sturdley shook his head. "I've got a pretty good eye for scale, measurement, that sort of thing. The guy I saw was a good twenty feet tall."

"Maybe he was on some kind of stilts or something," Peg offered.

"Climbing a sheer wall?" Sturdley asked. "Trust me, Red. That guy was for real."

The only sound in the office was the excited burbling from the radio. Both Peg and Harry sat in silence, each taking in what the other had just said.

The intercom on Peg's phone buzzed, startling them.

"Uh—uh, Peg?" It was Eddie Walcott, a young gopher who sometimes manned the reception desk. He sounded like he was talking from the bottom of a barrel over Peg's speakerphone. But his voice was cracking with suppressed excitement.

"What's up, Eddie?" Sturdley asked.

"Mr. S.—it's a camera crew from *First Person News*. They want to speak to, uh, you."

Sturdley glanced at Peg. Then he ran a hand through his hair. "Well, tell 'em to come right back."

Peg rose to her feet. "I'll get them."

Sturdley headed into his office. "And I'll get ready. Where's my jacket?"

Peg headed for reception to find a four-person TV crew led by an intense, rather thin, bleached-blond young newswoman. Hunched behind the desk was Eddie Walcott, staring at them with goggle eyes. He fell into the short-and-fat gopher variety, with a wide, flat face that Peg found rather froglike. Right now he looked like a frog that had just snagged something that didn't agree with him. Eddie's face was faintly green-tinged, and his pop-eyes were bigger than usual.

"I'm Ms. Faber, Mr. Sturdley's assistant," Peg said.

She got a quick, firm handshake. "Leslie Ann Nasotrudere." The newswoman already seemed "on," although her cameraman hadn't even unpacked his equipment. "We're here about the giants."

Peg gave her a wary look. "The ones tying up traffic on Fifth Avenue?"

"You know of any others?" Leslie Ann responded. "We were coming from downtown and couldn't get close. I consulted some sources and decided to come here. This has all the appearance of a comic-book plot, doesn't it? I spoke with Dirk Colby at Dynasty Comics. But he denied any knowledge or involvement, suggesting I call you."

Peg's eyebrows rose. "Well, I'm sure Mr. Sturdley will talk with you. Right this way."

She took the long route to Harry Sturdley's office, giving him as much time as possible to prepare. Stepping through his office doorway, she knocked gently. "Leslie Ann Nasotrudere of *First Person News*. She's here about the giants—Dirk Colby sent them."

Harry Sturdley was dressed for the press in a navy blazer and gray silk slacks. His cuffs were down, his tie was up, his hair was brushed and, Peg noticed, a picture of the Glamazon had appeared mysteriously behind his desk. Harry took the conversational ball Peg had handed him and ran with it.

"Dirk Colby sent you?"

The young newswoman nodded. "We thought perhaps this was one of Dynasty Comics' famous publicity stunts. I covered the demise of Zenith, the Man of Molybdenum. Mr. Colby assured us, however, that his company has nothing to do with these giants. If I can quote him off-record, he said, 'This sounds like some half-assed stunt like Harry Sturdley might try.'"

The news crew had set up by now, and Harry Sturdley was illuminated by floodlamps. A minicam pointed at him, and a microphone had appeared in Leslie Ann's hand.

"I regret to say, Leslie Ann, that we at the Fantasy Factory have no idea who the two giants are or where they may have come from."

Before the newswoman could cut the taping, Harry Sturdley reached out to take hold of the microphone.

"But judging from the reports we've gotten about them, how they stopped a crime in front of the Empire State Building, I think I can tell you *what* they are."

Peg glanced toward her desk. The portable radio was gone. The old fox must have been inside listening to it, getting as much information as he could.

"Well, what are they, Mr. Sturdley?" Leslie Ann Nasotrudere asked.

Happy Harry Sturdley smiled wide for the camera.

"They're Heroes," he said. "*Super*heroes."

CHAPTER 4

The giants spent the waning hours of the afternoon reconnoitering Central Park for a place to stay. For Robert, the parkland was a much-needed relief from pounding the pavement. Also, the wide-open spaces allowed him to outdistance the procession of Lessers that had been trailing them since he and Maurice had arrived on this world.

Throughout their march northward, Maurice had turned around every few intersections and made tentative shooing motions at the following they'd collected. The dark-haired giant had begun to get annoyed at the willfulness of the Lessers until Robert reminded his companion that these were, for all intents and purposes, untamed.

"They've much to learn," he'd said.

And so the giants beat an undignified retreat across the wide lawns of the park, leaving the crowd to tangle with the steadily growing numbers of officers in blue.

The problem was that no matter where they went, the giants quickly found a following. People wandering the park came to stare. Children asked their parents if this were a new ride. Countless cameras were snapped at the titans. Whenever they approached a road, traffic fell to a crawl as the Lessers operating these curious contraptions slowed down for a better look.

As the two zig-zagged through the park, they came upon a series of enclosures holding animals. The Lessers seemed to stare at the captive beasts with great interest until Maurice and Robert came along. Then they stared just as avidly at the giants.

"A zoo," Maurice picked up the concept from one of the watchers' minds. "That's what we're in now. This whole city—this entire world—is nothing more than a cage for us."

"Except that we have the opportunity to become the zookeepers," Robert pointed out, "a chance to exercise greater dominion than ever we had at home."

It was near darkness before they finally found a refuge in the southern part of the park, an area where the very bones of the bedrock poked through the earth to make a series of craggy slopes. One such rocky promontory jutted out into the waters of an ornamental pond. Few footpaths led through the area, protected as it was by water and sheer rock. Only on a short connecting neck of land was there a gentler slope, carpeted with rough greenery that finally extended down toward the manicured lawns to the north. The crown of the promontory had soil, and a copse of trees provided cover from curious eyes. Placed among the trees was a huge boulder, roughly oblong, with a flat top just the right height to provide a table for a kneeling giant.

Robert dug a toe into the matted softness of generations of leaves deposited on the soil. "I think this meets our needs," he said. "Comparative privacy, reasonable comfort—"

"And easily defensible," Maurice added, articulating a constant concern back at home.

"Against these Lessers?" Robert gave him a derisive smile.

Maurice shook his head and smiled back. "Old habits die hard."

"It's a good place." Robert leaned against the rock with a sigh and removed his buskins. To the south and east, he heard the constant susurrus of traffic, the uncountable hordes of Lesser ground-machines whirring on to their destinations. But here, for a moment, was the feeling of home.

Philly stumbled down the set of stairs hewn out of the rock, his arms raised to ward off blows. That was all he'd encountered in his life on the street, jeers and strong-arming for the skinny kid who "wasn't quite right in the head."

The homeless boy knew his defense wouldn't do any good. His arms and legs were like pipestems next to Ox, his tormenter. His only hope was to run. But Philly's long legs were clumsy. He tried to veer off the path and climb a steep, stony cliffside, but skidded on loose gravel and nearly went down on his butt.

His right arm was caught in a merciless grip—Ox had gotten him! Pain flared as Philly's captor twisted the arm at an unnatural angle. There was enough of Ox to make three Phillies. He was a big, misshapen blot of darkness as he hunkered over the kid. "Holdin' out on me, hah?" he growled, his breath a rank stench in Philly's face.

He smelled of spoiled food, bad wine, a handful of rotting teeth, greasy remnants caught in his tangle of unkempt beard. Ox boasted that he never washed—said it always got him a seat on the trains. Philly had seen the big man glom entire meals in fast-food joints, just by sitting across from a diner with a soda in his hand. People would abandon their meals with looks of disgust, and Ox would fall on their leavings with gusto.

Sometimes the big man would panhandle, but he preferred to scare money out of people. He'd find himself an isolated subway exit and pick his victims with care, smiling, offering to shake hands. Then he'd clamp onto the unwary passenger's hand with a vice-like grip, demanding their money.

Lately, he'd been charging Philly rent for sleeping space in the rustic summerhouse located on a nearby hilltop. Philly didn't know what a summerhouse was—he saw the place as a roof without much in the way of walls. But he remembered someone telling him that the park belonged to everybody. So why did Ox own the roof-place?

It had been good before Ox came here. People had even brought in old mattresses to sleep on. It was like a home.

But now Ox wanted money before he'd let you stay, and Philly had no money. He wasn't good at asking for it, not like the guys who paraded through the subway cars with their set little speeches. Horribly shy, not too bright, the best Philly could manage was a pleading look as people passed him by. It didn't bring in much. Today, there were just a few coins in his pocket. He'd had to raid trashbaskets for something to eat. He didn't have enough to pay Ox's rent.

Philly had decided not to sleep in the roof-place. It was warm enough, and dry enough, to bed down under a tree. But he'd left stuff in the place and went back to get it, and that's when Ox came after him.

"You owe me rent, ya little—" Ox pushed his face into Philly's, a gagging collection of stinks enveloping the kid from the bully's breath, skin, and clothes.

Philly didn't see the twisted, pock-marked face, the bulbous veiny nose. His eyes were tight shut, waiting for the beating to begin. He'd seen Ox kick a guy to death once. Nobody had said a thing about it.

His body was jolted, and he heard a heavy, crunching blow. But strangely, Philly felt nothing. A weird, bleating cry filled the air. It was Ox's voice, incredibly high pitched.

Philly opened his eyes. It was dark here in the gully between the hills, but he could make out the gigantic form looming over Ox. His nemesis looked like a baby compared to the newcomer—a scared baby.

Ox stood with his back against the rocky slope, drawn over to one side, his body twisted, one hand holding his ribs.

"Whaa—" he whined.

The dark, huge figure came toward him. "You annoy me, little man, with your physical stinks and your mind-stench. You could disappear and not one Lesser would care."

Drawing gasping breaths through his mouth, Ox tried to dart away. The giant swung in, slapping Ox with an open palm. Ox gave a bawl of agony as he was smashed against the rocks. Both arms now supported his ribs as he leaned against the stone. His breathing took on a bubbling tone.

With a sound of disgust, the giant raised a fist and brought it down. Philly heard something crunch, and a guttural rattle come from Ox's throat.

He stared up as the immense figure turned toward him, picking Philly out unerringly amid the shadows, crouching close enough that Philly could see the cold blue eyes, the blond hair.

Something stirred in Philly's memory, something he'd seen. A comic book with a giant in it. He'd protected people. This giant didn't match exactly. In Philly's recollection, the comic hero wore a bright yellow suit and a mask. But to Philly, it was all the same thing. "Bigman!" he cried, looking up at the handsome face above him.

Robert grimaced in reaction to the naked mind confronting him. This personality was so dissociated, there were hardly any shields at all. Feeling and images were broadcast willy-nilly. A picture invaded his immaterial senses; a gaudy image of an oversized hero in a bilious-colored costume.

"Bigman!" The small, slight figure below him repeated the name.

Robert unclenched his fist, repressing his immediate reaction to destroy so maimed a mind. He'd already acted hastily in killing the aggressor in the little drama he'd stumbled upon.

As Maurice said, he thought, *old habits die hard*.

Then Robert forced his way into the defenseless mind before him, easily overpowering the feeble consciousness there. He rifled the memories, expunging all traces of the death of the one called Ox. All that would remain was the recollection of meeting Bigman and being allowed to return to his place.

Robert pulled away his mental probes. He'd learned a considerable amount from this defective. It was worth a life. "Go back to your friends," he said. "Tell them that I will come to visit soon."

As soon as Philly had gone, Robert scooped up the crumpled body of Ox and brought it down to the pond. Along the banks, he'd noticed several large rocks. Prying one up, he set it aside, then put the body in the hollow the rock had covered. Water, mud, and other things squelched as Robert replaced the ten-foot stone and tamped it into place with his gigantic foot.

I wonder, he thought, *how difficult it would be to play the hero for less defective minds?*

Martyn Alexander Burke stretched naked in front of his bathroom mirror. He'd never forgiven his parents for sticking him with such a pretentious spelling on his first name—and such a stupid pronunciation— "Mah-TIN."

Growing up, the kids had called him something more like "Mawdy." Mawdy, the last kid to be picked on teams. Mawdy, the class nerd. Mawdy, who couldn't get a date in high school and college because he was too fat and drew superheroes in his notebooks.

Well, he'd shown them. He'd shown them all. Marty Burke was now a god to thousands of comic book fans across the country. He made some of the best money in the business, and women fell into his arms when they discovered they were in the presence of the writer and artist of *Mr. Pain,* the inventor of Schizodroid and M-16, Weapon Supreme. He'd come a long way from the fat kid working as a gofer for Harry Sturdley.

Automatically, Burke checked his waist for the

pudge factor and tightened his stomach muscles a little more. He'd lost weight thanks to the Fantasy Factory's starvation gofer wages and several lean years starting out as an artist. With success had come the constant temptation to pig out, now that he could afford to eat anything he wanted.

Was that why Sturdley had given Silicon Savage that eating disorder? To mock me, his top artist? He'd pay for that, along with all the other slights he'd piled on the new wave of artists Marty Burke was leading. Oh, the old man had been pretty hot stuff once, back in the sixties and seventies. But he was out of his depth in today's comics market, an obstacle on the path to the future of the Fantasy Factory—and Marty Burke.

The best thing Sturdley could do now was step down . . . before he got stepped on.

Burke frowned in the mirror, thinking back to the morning's staff meeting. He'd allowed himself to be outmaneuvered there. How could he handle *Mr. Pain* and the already delayed *Latter-Day Breed* while he was also supposed to be handling this *Death of the Glamazon* project?

No way he was letting go of *Breed*. That was something he'd developed from initial conception. It was all his, and he wasn't about to let anyone else in on the fan kudos and financial rewards to be reaped when the series finally hit the stands. As for the Glamazon thing, well, he'd already seen how eager that young snot Grantfield had been to horn in on a Marty Burke idea.

Doubtless Sturdley had noticed it, too. *If I don't keep on the project, Harry will use it as bait to turn my supporters into a pack of wild dogs, snapping at each other instead of bringing the old fox down.*

Reluctantly, Burke admitted to himself that temporarily he would have to give up *Mr. Pain*, right when the storyline was starting to get interesting. Sturdley would see to that.

Damn schedules. Damn Sturdley.

Burke sucked his gut in a little deeper.

He'd win. The force of history was behind him. The old must ever step aside for the young. And once he was in charge, he'd take these new so-called geniuses, the kids like Grantfield, down a peg or two.

Marty Burke smiled at his image in the mirror. Besides, now he had some outside aid—that blond TV reporter he'd met in the Fantasy Factory bullpen this afternoon. She'd been pretty steamed at the way Harry had manipulated her during his on-camera interview, especially since it meant she'd still have to take her crew in pursuit of the giants to get them on tape.

Leslie Ann Nasotrudere had been doing some desultory follow-up when he'd met her, and something had clicked. They'd exchanged cards, arranged a meeting . . .

"Marty?"

The female voice came through the bathroom door. "You've been in there a while. I'm beginning to wonder if you're no longer interested in . . . seconds."

Burke tightened his belly muscles again, then saluted his mirror image. Seconds on the dish in the bedroom should never be turned down. She was too tasty—too useful.

"Coming," he called, opening the door and turning down the short hall to the bedroom.

Kneeling among the black satin sheets, wearing

nothing more than her million-dollar smile, was Leslie Ann Nasotrudere.

"I think you can develop into a major contact," she purred.

"To new alliances," Burke said, climbing onto the bed. "And lots of contacts."

"Maybe we'll find a nice, rich yuppie on a bicycle," Cass Karolyk said to his friends. "Get us a set of wheels and a fat wallet."

"Not to mention a chance to kick some fat yuppie butt," Dolf Steiber added.

They entered the park at Eighty-sixth Street after a half-mile walk from the tenements near the East River—ten teenaged kids being pushed out of their own neighborhood. Once upon a time, the east Seventies and Eighties had been enclaves for immigrants from eastern Europe—Czechs, Hungarians, and Germans. Then it became a "desirable neighborhood"; old buildings were renovated into luxury residences, leaving less and less apartment space for the people who'd lived there. What had been a neighborhood became a scattering of ethnic restaurants, steadily being replaced by expensive clip-joints.

Names like Casimir and Adolf became jokes. And the owners of those names became steadily angrier and angrier.

Cass hefted the baseball bat in his right fist. Tonight there was going to be a little payback. The people who'd been pushing him and his friends around would find that the Bohunks and square-heads could fight back. And all the money in the world wouldn't help when he got his hands on them.

Central Park was different after sundown. The greens of the trees and grass faded to an indistinct gray, wanly lit here and there by a battered lamppost. Even the paths were dim and shadowy. Cass grinned in expectation. This would be his happy hunting ground.

An hour later, he was breathing heavily. He'd found himself a cyclist, but hadn't been able to catch the guy. One look at Cass and his crew, and the guy had begun pumping the pedals furiously. Cass had raced after him, trying to get in range. One swipe of his bat would knock the guy off the fancy leather saddle. Only problem was, he never got in swiping distance.

The guy on the bicycle headed out of the park at top speed, leaving Cass in the dust. Dolf looked dubious as their escaped prey crested a hill near the park exit. "What if he goes to the cops?" Dolf said.

"There's a whole lot of park, and only a few dumb cops," Cass said angrily, whacking the bat against the soles of his running shoes like a batter impatient for his turn at the plate. "We'll move off a little" he said, frustration making his gut almost as tight-clenched as his hand on the bat.

"Next person who comes along," he promised. "I don't care who they are. I bash first and ask questions later."

He heard the crunch of gravel in the distance, running footsteps—a jogger.

Crouched in the shadows, Cass twisted the bat back as if he were about to hit a home run. Here he came . . . here he came . . .

Cass got a glimpse of a pink headband, blond hair pulled back, rounded contours under a tank top. "He" was a she!

But the bat was already flashing toward her head. Cass had a quick glimpse of terrified features. A sick feeling filled his gut as he realized he couldn't stop his swing. His friends were closing in, hooting and yelling.

The female runner began to scream, and so, unbelievably, did the guys in the gang. Something big and dark came out of the shadows, moving inhumanly fast: a nightmare image of a huge hand swooping down to swat Cass' bat out of the way.

The enormous hand connected, sending Cass flying back to thud heavily into the grass and weeds. The bat bounced away, jarred from his hands.

The guys from the neighborhood scattered in terror, trying to escape whatever was after them. For a second, the impossible intruder was silhouetted against the glow of the distant streetlights, a gigantic human figure towering over them. The figure rushed forward, lazily swinging an arm. Cass could hear his friends' yelps and screeches as they stumbled all over themselves in the darkness, trying to escape.

Some headed across the path, hoping to lose themselves in the deeper shadows there. Instead, another massive block of darkness moved against the stars. Cass and his pals began yelling louder as the new attacker moved to block their retreat.

Cass got on his hands and knees, groping for his trusty bat. *The giants,* he thought. *It has to be those giants I saw on the tube.*

He rose to his feet and almost stumbled over the woman jogger. She was crumpled in a little ball on the ground, still screaming, even though she hadn't been hit. Cass felt bad about the screaming, but he was glad he hadn't connected. He didn't want to go smashing some girl's head.

That wasn't the problem now. The giants had apparently herded his friends away. He could hear the yelling, a little muffled by distance. With luck, Cass could just pull a fade.

At last his hands found the bat, and he started backing away. He wasn't sure exactly what was going on in the distance, and he didn't want to find out.

Ten steps, and Cass turned, intending to run for his life. Ahead of him, the night air was suddenly disturbed by what seemed to be a heavy breeze.

"You won't escape, Casimir," a deep voice boomed out of the darkness.

Cass tried to dart away, his body acting on autopilot as his mind froze. *He knows my name!*

"Don't bother running. I can see you, even in the dark."

Cass collided with something tree-like. But it was warm, smooth, fleshy. He'd bumped into the giant's leg.

Strictly on instinct, Cass brought up the bat to smash his way through the obstacle. His attack was directed against a massive, yard-wide shin.

The bat connected solidly. Even a guy with a hundred-and-thirty-inch chest should have felt that blow. Cass felt as if he'd hit a stone wall. The impact nearly jolted the bat from his grasp. But the giant stood there undisturbed, as if Cass were attacking him with a feather duster instead of a baseball bat. Fear and fury sent Cass over the edge. He battered away at the leg in a frenzy, determined to demolish it. Two, three killer blows landed right in the same spot. He should have cracked the shinbone.

No response.

Cass struck out at random, swinging wildly. He sent a swipe down at the ankle. He reached up to clout at the knee above his head. Minutes of futile bludgeoning continued, until sweat dripped down Cass Karolyk's corded muscles. His chest was heaving as if he'd run a mile, his breath came in ragged sobs. The bat wavered in his trembling arms. His muscles ached, and the palms of his hands stung as if the bones beneath the flesh were bruised.

What was the matter with this guy? Didn't he feel anything? Even if it took longer for pain to make its way up his brain, he should have felt it by now.

Cass raised his weapon for another faltering blow, but the giant finally lost patience. His weight shifted, and the leg Cass had been attacking moved. The titan's foot hooked around, dumping Cass flat on his butt.

The kid tried to scramble to his feet, only to flop face-first into some kind of hole in the grassy ground—a footprint, he foggily realized.

He'd just pushed himself up at arms' length when a huge hand came down out of the night to knock him flat again.

Cass squirmed on the ground. In the distance, he heard the wail of approaching sirens. The cops were coming! He had to get out of here!

Then two enormous hands whipped unerringly downward to smother Cass' wormlike motion. Cass Karolyk found himself helplessly pinned to the ground, the grass going up his nose.

"You're going nowhere, Cass," the deep voice overhead rumbled, "except to join your friends."

The giant hands scooped him up as if he were an infant. Cass rose up in the air—how high, he didn't know. They proceeded through the darkness to where the other giant waited near a lamppost beside a pile of still bodies.

"Th-they aren't—" Cass faltered.

"Your friends are only unconscious."

Cass looked up to see a stern, impossibly large yet handsome face staring down at him from under a mane of blond hair. "Why are you doing this?"

"The young woman down there could be asking the same question of you."

Huddled on the ground was the jogger Cass had almost brained with the bat. She had stopped screaming and now sat with her arms wrapped around her knees, looking at the ground. The woman seemed to be in shock.

Cass knew how she felt.

He was actually glad when the police arrived.

Cops I know how to deal with, Cass thought. *These guys . . . too weird, man.*

The law officers got out of their buzzing, beetle-like vehicles with weapons drawn to confront Robert and Maurice.

"What's going on here?" one of the older men demanded.

"These young ones tried to attack that woman," Robert said, pointing to the huddled young jogger. "We stopped them."

"It's like he says." The young woman finally found her voice. "That blond boy was going to smash me with a baseball bat. They saved me."

The officer pushed his hat to the back of his head.

"Start cuffing the punks," he said finally. "I think we'll take statements right here."

Minutes after the law officers arrived, larger, square-shaped vehicles pulled up. More of the Lessers emerged, carrying lights and strange box-like contraptions on their shoulders.

A quick mental scan told Robert that these were newsgatherers. The boxes and sticks some of them held somehow recorded sounds and images. After having discussed things mind-to-mind with Maurice, he was prepared to speak. "We are strangers here," he said to the tiny recorders, "wanderers in a strange land. But we can see when evil is done, when crimes are committed. This we cannot allow."

The Lessers' response was a cacophony of questions. Robert answered to the best of his ability, ending with a solemn promise: "Wherever we find wrongdoing going on, we *will* intervene."

At last, there were no more questions. The lawbreakers had been taken away, as had the victim. Now the newsgatherers and the law officers left, as well.

Maurice shook his head in admiration. "You handled that perfectly, Robert. Better than I could have. How eager these Lesser are to have someone protect them!"

His eyes drilled into the darkness, an intangible probe going far beyond human sight, to locate someone skulking in the shadows. A wisp of thought from the skulker identified him as a petty malefactor.

Maurice stepped into the glow of the lamplight, still staring into the darkness. Now he pointed at the would-be thief. "OUT!" he roared, his voice echoing across the rolling lawns.

A very startled mugger took to his heels.

Maurice turned to his companion, his face glowing. "This is wonderful!" He looked down at his hands, to the ground below, then off to the buildings in the distance. "It seems that I can search, and hear thoughts, even more clearly than at home."

Robert nodded. "I think that our passage from the world we know to this one somehow sharpened our mind-powers." He smiled. "All the better. I've been trying to search out the one who brought us here. I can't find him among all these other minds, but I've located where he was. That I will look into tomorrow."

Maurice looked surprise. "Why look for the one who brought us? You've already said you don't want to go back."

"Oh, I intend to stay," Robert agreed. "But if we are really to settle here, we'll need more of our kind." Once again, he realized, Maurice hadn't thought of the future at all.

"We'll need females of our own race to perpetuate ourselves," Robert pointed out patiently. "And as far as we know, there's only one person on this world who can bring them to us."

"Will he?" Maurice asked.

"I don't know," Robert answered. "I can't even tell you why he brought us here."

The giant frowned into the darkness, spreading his powers wide. "But I intend to know before the sun goes down tomorrow."

CHAPTER 5

Gerald Carlyle wasn't used to rising at five A.M. He probably hadn't been up as early as this since his starting-out days, when he'd made the commute from Queens to the Newark office of the firm. That was a good twenty years ago, long before he'd become a partner . . . back when he could still see his toes.

Becoming forty had hit Jerry Carlyle like a ton of bricks—most of which had stuck around his middle. He'd gone through two new wardrobes in the past three years while his body had seemed to inflate madly. It had been hard to play the take-charge, roll-up-the-sleeves type when removing his jacket revealed a big roll of flab hanging over his waistband, making a mockery of his silk executive suspenders.

He'd finally had to admit his blimpishness when he'd found himself panting after bending over to tie a shoelace.

That, and the realization that fat boys don't make partner-in-charge, had impelled Jerry Carlyle to a decision. He'd have to exercise.

Jerry moved logically along to the next questions: *where?* and *how?* His first thought was a fat farm, but he couldn't take the time. And health clubs were out of the question. He had no wish to be seen and commented on.

In the end, he'd found only one combination that promised exercise and anonymity: a daily jog around the reservoir in Central Park, accomplished at the crack of dawn.

Groaning, Jerry Carlyle stumbled out of bed, threw some water in his face, and surveyed the world with bleary eyes. Arrayed on the kitchen table were his preparations—a set of sweats, size extra-large, and a handful of vitamins and mineral supplements. He washed the pills down with a glass of half orange juice, half water (so it wouldn't be so acid on an empty stomach), and set off.

The East Side was another world in the pre-dawn gloom. Jerry could feel the slowly growing brilliance on the horizon behind him as he headed for the park.

He entered just north of the Metropolitan Museum of Art, crossed the nearly deserted Park Drive East, and finally reached the jogging track around the manmade lake that had once served as the main outlet for Manhattan's drinking water. By that time, he was already puffing. And he still faced the two-mile jog around the reservoir itself.

Jerry had plodded perhaps halfway round the lake. The good thing was that there was no one to see his agonizing progress. Not that he was looking around. His eyes were glued to the surface of the track as he forced one clumsy foot in front of the other.

He didn't even notice the sloshing sound until it was

repeated two or three times. Wheezing almost asthmatically, Jerry finally raised his gaze and come to a halt. His eyes went wide when he realized there was a figure slicing across the water of the reservoir. What could it be? A seal? A whale? The Loch Ness Monster?

Whatever it was, the figure seemed to be heading toward the spot where Jerry was standing. He began jogging again, with considerably more speed. His watery pursuer changed course to intercept farther along the jogging path, reached the shore, and abruptly rose up to reveal itself as a twenty-foot-tall naked man.

Jerry Carlyle's mouth popped open, his eyes popped out, and, apparently, his heart did, too. Something burst in his chest. He managed three more steps before he keeled over.

Standing over the still form, in fact, dripping water on it, Maurice monitored the arrhythmic heartbeat with his immaterial senses. Casting about, he Searched for the nearest place of healing and picked up the unconscious Gerald Carlyle. He paused a moment to get his clout, and set off.

When Harry Sturdley woke up the next morning, every station in town seemed to be playing up the giants' overnight crime-fighting exploits, plus the early-morning rescue. *First News in the Morning* also played the clip with Harry calling them "heroes." They'd played it the night before, too.

Harry hailed a cab to take him to the office. The driver was listening to a commentator on one of the city's all-news radio stations: "New York has faced a shortage of giants in the last few years. The baseball Giants deserted the Polo Grounds for San Francisco more than three decades ago. The football Giants headed off to a stadium in New Jersey. We began to doubt if we really were the greatest city in the world. Maybe we'd become a city of pygmies.

"Well, we don't have to worry anymore. The newest New York Giants are just what this city needs."

Harry was pleased. The morning papers he'd picked up were also calling the giants "Heroes." The *Post* had run a pithy headline:

GIANTS 10

PUNKS 0

"So what do you think about these giants?" Sturdley asked the cabdriver as they headed downtown.

The cabbie, an elderly Jewish guy, only grinned. "Last time I heard good things about giants, Bobby Thompson hit the homer back in 1951. It broke my heart—I'm a Brooklyn kid. I hope these giants treat me better."

Sturdley smiled. Here at last were real-life, hometown heroes, and he was determined that the Fantasy Factory would be doing the comic books. Only two unanswered questions kept Harry from being fully happy: Where the hell did these guys come from? And did they already have an agent?

The cab pulled up at his office building, and Sturdley got out. Halfway across the lobby, he was accosted by a tall, stooped figure in a frayed tweed coat. "Harry?"

Sturdley turned to see a mournful, thin face with a beak of a nose and thinning gray hair. Mack Nagel looked like a caricature of his own work. The guy used to draw for the old horror comics, creating dapper if threadbare anthology hosts in his own image. They were all tall and beaky-nosed, with elegant black frock coats going slightly to seed. But Nagel's eyes weren't deep-set and evil; they were only tired and imploring.

"I hate to beg like this, Harry. But I need some work."

I should have guessed it, Sturdley thought. *The poor guy probably hasn't had a regular gig in years.*

"I wouldn't ask for myself," Nagel went on, "but my wife's sick. Nancy was always such good friends with your Myra—"

"Come on upstairs," Sturdley said with a nod. "I'll see if we can't find something for you."

"Anything," Nagel said. "I know my art style doesn't jibe with what your young guys are doing, but I can do page breakdowns. People always liked my layout abilities."

"Let's go and have a look around," Sturdley said, leading the older artist into the elevator. As the doors closed, he asked, "How are you at drawing giants?"

They arrived on the third floor, and Sturdley led the way into the offices. He paused for a second, debating whether to head for the executive wing or the bullpen. Then he saw Bob Gunnar coming down the hall. Sturdley stepped ahead, beckoning to his lanky number-two man. "Bob, do you know Mack Nagel? I'm sure you've seen his work on the old *Spine-Tingling Stories*."

Gunnar's eyebrows went up as he whispered to Harry, "I thought he was dead." Then he shook Nagel's hand and said, "Well, a few of the younger guys could use some layout help. Zeb Grantfield's getting behind schedule on *Jumboy*."

"From the *Sensational Six*?" Nagel said.

"Yeah," Sturdley said, handing Nagel off to Gunnar. "Worst attitude of the group, but the fans love him. We've split him off for his own book. He's twelve feet tall in the spin-off." He grinned. "Good practice for drawing giants."

Gunnar had started to lead Nagel off to the bullpen. Now he stopped in the middle of the hallway. "Giants?" he asked.

"Just a possible project I'd like to explore," Sturdley responded airily. He headed down the hallway to the executive offices. Zeb Grantfield was leaning over Peg Faber's desk. She was staring in disbelief as he showed her the latest page he was working on. "That's me?" she asked in a bemused voice.

Sturdley came up and glanced at the drawing. It was a typical Grantfield woman: big chest, small hips, clenched teeth, and no pupils in the eyes. "Zeb, I don't think you caught the essential Peg," he said.

Grantfield whirled around as if he'd been caught with his hand in the cookie jar. He was tall and gawky, with the intensity of a Kubert hero. Of course, Kubert wouldn't draw in the zits and acne scars. They would fade, once Grantfield got a little farther away from twenty.

"I heard you're running a little late on *Jumboy*," Sturdley said.

The surprised Grantfield opened and closed his mouth a few times, reminding Sturdley of a fish out of water. He didn't give the kid a chance to frame an answer. "So I got some layout help for you—Mack Nagel. Know who he is?"

Grantfield might be surprised, but he knew his comics. *"Spine-Tingling Stories."*

Sturdley nodded. "The man's an unheralded genius. I hope you'll appreciate what I'm doing for you."

Zeb Grantfield nodded and beat a hasty retreat toward his office near the bullpen.

Peg smothered a smile. "Well, you sure put the fear of the Lord into him," she said.

"Kid can't draw without photo reference," Sturdley snorted. "Hell, he couldn't get *you* right, and you're right down the hall from him."

Peg glanced down at the thick cotton sweater she was wearing. "Well, I don't usually come to work in a skintight unitard."

"Thank God, or we'd never get any work done," Sturdley replied. "What's on the schedule for today?"

"You're spending the morning with Gunnar and a couple of artists, discussing image changes for some of our older characters."

Sturdley nodded. "Where are we meeting?"

"In the conference room. Gunnar didn't want you messing up your office if you started throwing things."

"That was yesterday," Sturdley told Peg. "I'm a new man today." He thought for a second. "Get McManus down in Legal. I want to find out what the restrictions are concerning comic books about living people."

Peg raised her eyebrows but said nothing as Sturdley headed down the hallway to the conference room.

"Okay, who's next on the schedule?" Sturdley asked, shifting through the pile of illustration boards on the middle of the table. He held up a pen-and-ink portrait of a young woman with almond-shaped eyes and high cheekbones. She wore a cheongsam, the traditional dragon-lady style dress. The skirt came down to her ankles, but was slit up to her hipbone. The neckline was modest, but a huge pearl pendant rode in the cleft between her breasts. The woman's black hair was pulled up in a bun.

"Okay, this is the old look for the Yellow Pearl, the Human Torpedo's Japanese nemesis from World War II," Gunnar said.

"Actually," Jim Pickett, one of the artists sitting in on the meeting broke in, "she's the *granddaughter* of the original Yellow Pearl. I mean, the original would have to get older while the Human Torpedo was trapped in suspended animation in that sunken submarine . . ."

"All right, all right," Sturdley snapped. *These blasted boy artists think they invented story continuity,* he thought. "We wanted to change her image because we were getting some flak about the political correctness of calling an Oriental villain 'yellow'—" Sturdley began.

"Asian," Reece Yantsey, one of the other artists, said.

"What?"

"It's politically incorrect to call *Asian* people *Orientals,*" Yantsey explained. "They prefer—"

"When I think what we used to call them back in World War II, they should be glad we call them Orientals," Sturdley grumped. "So what have we named this character now?"

"Just 'the Pearl,'" Gunnar said. "She still has the same basic powers—part mad scientist, part witch."

"And what's the proposal for the new look?" Sturdley said.

Pickett reached into his portfolio and drew out a new piece of illustration board. There was a woman with the same facial features, but the rest was completely different. Her hair was now a black nimbus around her head. The cheongsam was gone, replaced by what appeared to be a translucent baby-doll top with a pair of thong bikini bottoms. The pearl pendant still dangled between the character's breasts, but now the breasts were bigger, the hips smaller, and the pupils had disappeared from her eyes.

"I figure this brings her into the nineties," Pickett said. "And it gets rid of the whole Asian look."

"By getting rid of most of her clothes," Sturdley commented.

"Let's face it, Harry," Gunnar said. "There's political correctness, and then there's sales."

"Okay," Sturdley said. "Just do me one favor."

"What's that?" Pickett asked.

"Can the Grantfield eyes. Give her some pupils."

They moved on to the next character. Gunnar picked up the picture, a two-figure study of a thin, dignified man in a lab coat and an enormous diapered baby stamping his foot. "The Petulant Lump has been a staple character since the sixties," he began. "As we all know, Dr. Wayne Walters took a super-soldier serum that failed. Now he turns into a seven-foot-tall baby—the Lump—whenever he gets pissed off."

"I think the world is *petulant*," Sturdley said.

"The problem is to figure how to make the Lump's image up-to-date," Gunnar said.

"I think he needs to get a little tougher," Reece Yantsey said. "How about this?"

His picture was the same old Lump—except the diaper was now made of camouflage cloth. "The Rambo look, get it?"

"I've got an idea along those lines," said another of the young artists, Xan Ximenes. He held up a pencil sketch, just a head shot of the Lump—scowling over a two-day's growth of beard.

Gunnar looked dumbfounded. "He's supposed to be a baby. How could he grow a beard?"

"Yeah, but he looks interesting that way," Sturdley said. "All we need is a way to make it work."

He suddenly snapped his fingers. "Suppose we give Walters a beard. That way, the facial hair will be there already."

Pencils hit sketchpads, coming up with new versions of Wayne Walters' face.

They were interrupted as the door to the conference room swung open, revealing Peg Faber. "Harry, there's someone here to see you." Her gray eyes were enormous in a pale face.

"We're in the middle of a meeting, Peg," Sturdley said testily.

"Yes, but this is—big." An almost hysterical laugh came from her lips.

Sturdley frowned, turning back to the set of drawings. "Well, whoever it is will have to wait in my office."

"He can't—won't fit." Another set of giggles escaped from Peg. Then she explained. "I was at my desk, and I heard a tapping at your window."

"My window?" Sturdley repeated. "That's three stories above the ground. Nobody could reach—"

"Two people now in town could reach it," Peg said in a strangled voice. "This one's name is Robert."

Sturdley's jaw dropped. "You mean one of the giants is *here*—and he wants to see me?"

Peg nodded. "He's standing outside your window right now."

"Meeting adjourned!" Sturdley shot to his feet and was out of the conference room as if he'd been fired from a gun. He dashed down the hall to his office, burst through the doorway, and nearly flung himself out the window. Once there, however, he pulled himself back.

Oh, he'd seen three-foot-tall heads before. He had a projection-system TV at home. But it was one thing to see a close-up on a screen, and quite another to see the same thing in the flesh.

The giant was a perfect specimen, an Alex Raymond hero brought to life—even to the golden hair.

"You are Sturdley," the giant said, aiming piercing blue eyes in Harry's direction. They seemed to burn right into his brain, then widened in surprise. "You felt it," Robert burst out. "You felt the shock of our coming here."

"I did?" Sturdley said in bafflement. Then it struck him. That moment yesterday, when the bottom fell out of the world, when he wound up gasping and clutching at Peg's desk. Oddly, Sturdley felt relief—it hadn't been a heart attack.

"I see it in you even now," Robert said. "Yet I see no reason, even though your servant is the one who brought us over."

"My servant?" Now Sturdley was completely lost.

"The one who serves you here." Robert glared piercingly at Sturdley, but his mental powers didn't tell him what he wanted.

He was forced to explain.

"The one you call John," Robert said. "John Cameron."

CHAPTER 6

"John Cameron?" Harry Sturdley echoed stupidly. "You want John Cameron?"

"He *is* your servant," Robert the giant said pointedly.

For a brief second, Sturdley had the mental image of John Cameron in a butler's suit. He pushed the picture out of his head, still trying to find his mental footing. "The kid works for me, yes, but that doesn't make him my servant." Sturdley's eyes narrowed. "What do you want him for?"

"We need him if we are to succeed."

"Succeed?"

The giant nodded.

"All I can say is you're not making sense. Start it off simply, from the beginning."

Robert scowled, glaring at Sturdley, but he apparently saw that the man in the window was sincere in his ignorance.

"Maurice and I did not come to this world by our own efforts," Robert said, picking his words with care.

"We were brought here. And your worker, John Cameron, is the one who summoned us."

Sturdley's face was a mask of disbelief. "How do you know the kid pulled this off?"

"The fact that I am here is proof enough for me," Robert said. "One moment, I was on my home world. The next, I felt a terrible twisting sensation. It was as if a rift had opened beneath my feet. I seemed to fall through a tremendous void. While that was happening—" Sharp blue eyes shot a glance to Sturdley. "You know that my people can communicate mind-to-mind?"

Sturdley didn't know, but he nodded anyway.

"While I was in the void, I Searched—sent out my mental probes. They connected with one other mind— John Cameron's. Then I abruptly found myself on your world."

Harry Sturdley's fingers tightened on the window casement. Robert had described the same symptoms he'd experienced in that weird fit he'd had. And then, moments later, he'd seen the giant climbing the Empire State Building.

His thought was interrupted by a loud, low rumble, the bodily sounds of hunger.

"Have you eaten anything since you got here?" Sturdley asked abruptly.

"No," Robert admitted.

"Stay there."

Sturdley whirled toward his doorway, only to discover he had an audience. Peg Faber had turned her chair and was staring at the scene by the window. Standing behind her were Elvio Vital and Marty Burke.

Yes, even the imperturbable Marty the Genius was spellbound by the gargantuan presence.

"I've got a starving giant out there," Sturdley said. "Here's what I want. You," he pointed at Vital, "go get three dozen bagels with lox, half with cream cheese, half with butter. You"—he now pointed to Burke—"I want enough coffee to fill that thermos decanter on my desk."

Burke came back to earth with a thump of injured dignity. "I'm no gofer—" he began.

Sturdley brutally cut him off. "I'm trying to make a *deal* with this guy. The biggest deal this company will ever make. And if you screw it up, I'll make sure the whole world knows who's responsible."

Burke shut his mouth with an audible snap. "Getting coffee," he grated. Then, gesturing curtly toward Peg Faber, he demanded, "Why can't she—?"

"I've got another job for Peg," Sturdley answered, facing his assistant. "Go find John Cameron and bring him here *pronto*."

Sturdley turned back to the window. He was up against a twenty-foot giant who apparently could read minds. But the giant needed something that Harry Sturdley controlled, and that gave Sturdley a negotiating edge.

And Sturdley intended to negotiate for all he was worth. He was as curious as all New Yorkers about the mysterious giants, and he had a thousand questions he'd love to ask. He also had a plan, and now was not the time to get sidetracked.

"I've asked my people to rustle up something for you to eat," he said to the giant. "That's a problem you'll have to face on this world. It's also something I could help you with." He glanced shrewdly up into the giant's face. "So what exactly have you got in mind for getting along here?"

"I have seen the fear of the people in this city—and probably this world. Apprehension over crime weighs everything they do. My companion and I have the power to fight crime and end that fear."

He wants to become a crime-fighter, Sturdley thought. *This is almost too good to be true.*

"You'll need help—someone who knows this world and how it ticks." Sturdley permitted himself a smile. "Someone who understands your needs and can help keep you fed."

"I don't sense a deep charitable purpose behind your words," Robert said. "You're some kind of merchant and hope to make a profit."

"I sell comic books—picture stories of heroic action. They're read by almost every child and many adults in our society. My heroes share your goals, but they're fiction—they aren't real. Your heroics can make those goals come true. As related in my comics, they'll inspire the nation, fill our people with awe and respect for you and your friend. I'll need a contract with the two of you, giving me the sole rights to sell—I mean, *tell*—your adventures. A full licensing agreement."

"You can have that, and gladly—if Maurice and I can have what we need."

"And that is?" A disquieting thought came to Sturdley. What if the two giants wanted *out*? What if the only reason they want John Cameron is that he's their only ticket home?

Robert must have caught the thought, because he

shook his head. "We wish to stay on this world. It offers us more scope than the place we came from."

He glanced down at his perfectly formed body. "But we do want the company of our own kind. If we are to live out our lives here . . ."

The giant looked up, a wry smile pulling at his handsome features. "I am not ill-formed, Sturdley. But I doubt I could attract any of your women."

"There would be a question of size," Sturdley had to admit.

"We wish to bring more of our people over—enough to give us fifty in this world," Robert said. "Half of them female."

He made an expansive gesture. "If you and John Cameron will help us in this, we will sign this licensing agreement of yours."

"The other of your kind will have to be bound by it, too," Sturdley quickly said. "I don't want anybody brought over who starts making side deals with my competitors."

The giant's eyes took on a steely glint. "I guarantee that all will abide by our agreement."

"Then I think we can do business," Sturdley said, savoring the moment of triumph. He heard bustling in the corridor outside his office and turned to see Elvio Vital entering with a heavy shopping bag.

"I got the largest ones they had," the artist said, holding out the package.

Behind him was Marty Burke, carrying a full pot of coffee. "You owe me for expenses, Sturdley. I had to shell out and buy the whole damn pot from the deli downstairs."

"As long as you got it," Sturdley said. "Just bill us."

He opened the vacuum-sealed decanter on his desk and filled it with fresh coffee. "Have we got milk and sugar?"

Swearing, Burke stepped away from the door.

"We have some in the bullpen," Elvio Vital said, his sense of hospitality taking over. "I'll get it."

Sturdley opened the bag of bagels and started arranging them on the windowsill beside the decanter. "This is what we often have for breakfast," he told the giant. "Do you have coffee where you come from?"

Robert carefully removed the thermos pitcher. Two of his fingers fit inside the handle, like a coffee mug. He sniffed the rising steam and wrinkled his nose. "This is new to me," Robert admitted.

"Lots of people add milk and sugar," Sturdley explained. "We'll have them in a minute."

And I hope we'll have John Cameron to talk to, as well, he went on silently, shaking his head. It was hard to believe that the kid had a central part to play in this whole bizarre business. Or was it? He'd always thought the kid was only visiting planet Earth. Maybe his impression was more accurate than he'd imagined.

The doorway filled again, but it was just Vital with the cream and sugar. Where were Peg and John Cameron?

Robert had made half the bagels disappear before Peg finally appeared in the doorway—alone.

"Harry, he's not here," she said. "I've just checked both floors and asked all the guys in the bullpen in case somebody sent him out for something. It looks as though John Cameron didn't show up today."

Sturdley smacked his forehead, then turned back to the window. Before he could explain things to Robert, the giant cut him off. "I already know that your worker is not in this building. But you must find him for me . . . or we have no deal."

Happy Harry ground his teeth, then said to Peg, "Get the kid on the horn."

Peg held up a sheet of paper—John Cameron's employment form. "He hasn't got a phone, Harry."

"Tell you what," Sturdley said to Robert, determined to keep the deal alive. "I'll send up breakfast for your friend Maurice—keep you both fed as a gesture of my good faith. I'll advise you, too. There are subtleties to being a successful superhero in this world. You've got to keep the media on your side, for one thing, or they'll turn the people against you. I can help with that."

"That would eliminate two worries," Robert admitted. "I'll abide by our spoken agreement, Sturdley."

"Good, good," Harry said. "I'll have one of my people meet you downstairs with more supplies."

He headed to the doorway. A large crowd had now gathered by the entrance to his office. Harry dug a twenty-dollar bill out of his pocket and gave it to a gaping gofer. "Get more coffee and bagels for the big guy to take with him."

Then he turned to those at the front of the crowd—Peg, Burke, and Elvio Vital. "You three get to where Cameron lives. Where the hell is it?"

Marty Burke had the form in his hand. "Someplace called Astoria. Where's that?" he asked in his most haughty voice.

Sturdley snatched it, looked, then raised his eyes to the heavens. "Great. The kid lives in Queens. I want you to track him down and get him in here."

Burke drew himself up to his full height. "Me, too, Harry?"

Sturdley looked at his stiff-necked rival, then allowed himself a smile. "Yeah, I want you to go, too, Marty."

Sturdley handed Peg the form, then raked the other crowd members with a glare. "Haven't the rest of you got work to do?" he barked.

Ten minutes later, his gofer returned with two bulging shopping bags. Harry took them, headed for the window, and then stopped. He opened one bag and sniffed. The look he aimed at the hapless kid could have melted steel.

"*Onions?*" he said, making the word sound like a terrible obscenity. "You got bagels with lox and *onions?* How do you know they agree with our large friend out there? You want to give him indigestion—or the trots? Do I have to do the thinking for everyone around here?" Grimacing, Harry quickly began opening the bagels to remove the large rings of Bermuda onion placed inside. In his hurry, he wound up smearing cream cheese on his shirt cuffs, his suit jacket, even his tie.

"The things I do for this company," he fumed.

"The things I do for this company," Peg Faber muttered to herself as she got onto the elevator. She had heard the strange bargaining going on through Harry's window, and the incredible reason why John Cameron was wanted. Frankly, she felt uncomfortable going to round him up.

In an office where almost every male had tried to pick her up—or looked at her the way a hungry dog eyes a piece of meat—John Cameron was the only one who had kept his distance.

Oh, he was perfectly nice and friendly. He just didn't flirt, tell dirty jokes, or try to look down her blouse. John Cameron acted like a gentleman, which was a rather foreign experience in the rowdy atmosphere of the Fantasy Factory.

And now she was chasing him.

Peg led the artists across the lobby, to find the Park Avenue traffic hopelessly snarled up thanks to the giant's passage. "We'll be stuck here all day," she said, walking east.

Marty Burke tried not to let his satisfaction show as he allowed the girl to lead him over to Third Avenue. He'd put one over on Harry Sturdley, maneuvering him into ordering him onto this Cameron hunt. That could mean some leverage for him around deadline time. The hunt could also help with Leslie Ann Nasotrudere. Last night, she'd asked him to keep an eye out for anything strange going on at the Fantasy Factory. Sturdley's weird deal with the giants certainly rated as that. Inside knowledge equaled power. The ability to broadcast that information equaled more power. He'd have to keep the others from realizing how pleased he was.

They managed to catch a northbound cab a moment after they reached Third Avenue. "You should've gotten some petty cash to take care of this," Burke complained.

Peg couldn't believe her ears. Here was a guy who made thousands in royalties every month from *Mr. Pain* alone, grousing over the cabfare to Queens.

"I'll put in for expenses when we get back," she said.

Astoria, Queens, was an old neighborhood with numerous brick apartment buildings, now inhabited by a melting pot of ethnic groups. The directory of the building that John Cameron gave as home was a regular league of nations. The first six buzzer buttons yielded names as diverse as McLaughlin, Georgiou, Gupta, Fong, Santiago, and a wayward Smith. None of the labels had a "Cameron" on it.

"Is there an apartment number on that form?" Burke asked in annoyance.

Peg squinted at the piece of paper in her hand. The handwriting was a tiny scrawl, nearly illegible. "Yes, 4-B. He put it in the wrong space."

Apartment 4-B was occupied by a family named Putnik. Peg pushed the buzzer, and a second later, a cracked voice responded in a language she didn't know.

"What the hell is she saying?" Burke groused.

"It's not Spanish," Elvio said with a shrug.

The voice on the intercom grew sharper, though still incomprehensible.

"John Cameron," Peg said into the speaker.

"Who you?" the voice came back.

"We want John Cameron," Peg said.

"You come up." The door buzzed, and the three of them entered. There was no elevator, so they started up the stairs.

"What language do you think she was talking?" Burke wondered.

"From the name and the sound of it, something like Carpathian," Peg said.

Elvio Vital's eyebrows rose. "You speak Carpathian?"

"No," Peg said. "But I had to proofread all the Carpathian place names and words that got used in the Vampire Wars storyline in *Ex-Wives*."

"That rag," Burke scoffed. "Who'd be interested in a bunch of bitchy ex-wives of superheroes who got their powers through a sexually transmitted disease?"

"Do I sense a little bit of jealousy, Burke? I hear that *Ex-Wives* outsells even *Mr. Pain*."

"That's because Grantfield used to do it," Burke grumped. "People bought it because he draws big boobs."

They reached the fourth floor. Apartment 4-B was right by the stairwell.

On the first knock, the door opened to reveal a European grandmother type in a tobacco-colored sweater and a bubushka.

"You know John?" The woman made the name sound more like "Yahn."

Peg nodded.

"He in his room." The woman jerked a thumb over her shoulder. "No come out."

"I was wondering how young John could afford a place," Elvio said. "Now I see—he rents one room."

"Rent!" the elderly woman seized on the word. "He no pay. We wait. He no come out. Not even go to bathroom." That came out more like "bat-room."

Peg began to get concerned. "How long?" she asked.

"A day. We wait. We watch. My Draghi, he up all night. No John."

"We'd better check this out." Peg looked down the hallway. "Which is John's room?"

The woman pointed to a heavily painted door at the end of the hallway.

Peg ran to the door, knocking on it. "John? It's Peg Faber, from work."

No answer.

She knocked harder, her knuckles ringing against the heavy green paint. "John, we know you're in there. Answer me, please!"

When no response came this time, she turned in desperation to the two artists. "I think something is wrong."

"I'll get in." Burke gestured her out of the way, then took a running start from down the hall and rammed into the door. He bounced back with a yell, rubbing a sore shoulder.

"Dunno what's wrong with this stupid door," he complained.

"John!" Peg yelled, beginning to get frightened.

Elvio Vital placed himself with his back to the door. He brought up his right leg and kicked backward, right under the doorknob. Twice, three times—until suddenly the lock gave.

The door flew open and Peg dashed inside, calling John Cameron's name.

It was a long, thin, airless space, more like a walk-in closet than a room. Along one wall, an army cot was set up, with sheets and blankets neatly folded on top.

Lined up on the other wall was a dresser and a floor-to-ceiling arrangement of long cardboard boxes. Peg recognized them immediately as comics storage boxes—John's comics collection.

Elvio gravitated to the end of the room by the window, where a large picture of a flying hero was tacked to a drawing board. "I didn't know the kid drew," he said. "Say, this is pretty good."

"Probably tracing somebody else's stuff on a lightbox," Burke crabbed.

"I don't see a lightbox in here," Elvio said. His shaggy eyebrows rose. "And I don't see John."

Peg had already come to that conclusion. The only available hiding place was under the bed. She'd already checked there, coming up with an unmatched sock. "Where is he? The woman said the door was watched all night." Peg dusted her hands.

"Maybe he was skipping on his rent. He wouldn't use the door." Burke sounded like quite an expert. Peg wondered if he'd ever skipped on his rent.

The stocky artist went to the window. "*This* would be the route he'd take."

Burke took hold of the handle and tried to throw the window open. His hand slipped off, but the window didn't move. He tried again, grunting with effort. The window didn't budge.

"Must be locked," he said.

"Doesn't need a lock," Elvio Vital said, running a hand along the side of the window frame. "Look."

Generations of paint had welded the old window to its sill.

"It hasn't been opened," Peg said, bending to stare at the fossilized paint.

Then she stood up and scratched her head. "So where is he?"

CHAPTER 7

Harry Sturdley sat uncomfortably in the cab, setting out for the strangest luncheon meeting of his career. For one thing, he wasn't exactly sure where it would be. For another, he was bringing the lunch.

In the trunk were fifteen pounds of deli sandwiches, gaily wrapped in red plastic, along with tubs of condiments and salads, plus a cooler full of drinks.

His destination was the Maine Monument, at the southwestern corner of Central Park. Judging from the way traffic was crawling up Eighth Avenue, one or both of the giants must be waiting for him already.

When they reached the southern end of Columbus Circle, Harry could see a dark-haired figure rising up at least as tall as the monument itself. "Let me off here," he said, paying the cabbie. "And pop the trunk." Then, balancing his ungainly load, he set off across the traffic circle on foot.

Normally, that would have been risky in the extreme, as it meant braving vehicles roaring along Broadway, Eight Avenue, Central Park West, and Fifty-ninth

Street. However, the rubber-neckers by the park had screwed up traffic sufficiently that nothing was moving. Sturdley only had to zig-zag his way between virtually parked cars. The only damage he risked was to his eardrums from the honking horns and the swearing of the stranded drivers.

At last, he reached the corner of the park. Then all he had to do was push his way through the ring of bystanders gaping up at the giant. They were of all kinds and colors, from Japanese tourists snapping rolls of film to raggedy street people. An irregular empty circle surrounded the base of the monument where Maurice stood. Beyond that rippled a jammed human wall feeding their curiosity.

If I ever needed convincing proof that we're descended from monkeys, here it is, Sturdley thought.

He pressed on to the only open space in the crowd, where a dog-walker tried to control a half-dozen yapping charges that yanked at their leashes, trying to lunge at the huge figure.

The crowd shifted as a pair of harassed cops tried to keep people from pressing closer. "Stay back, now," one cop said. "Haven't you seen enough now? Why don't you move on."

For every person who tried to shift away, however, two more pushed forward. The cop, who to Harry's eyes looked like a high school junior who'd been outfitted for a stage play, tilted back a hat that was slightly too large.

"Look, uh—"

"Maurice," the giant said obligingly.

"Yeah, Maurice. You're tying up traffic and blocking

the sidewalk. I can't let you stay here." The young cop's voice took on a distinct whine.

Let? Sturdley compared the giant to the skinny blue-clad kid who barely came up to Sturdley's shoulder. No question about who was the authority figure here. Juggling his burdens, Harry stumbled around dog leads to reach the front of the crowd.

An ambitious pretzel vendor who'd set his wagon up front frowned at the apparent food competition. "Giddadheah," he yelled. "This is my corner."

"Maurice!" Sturdley called up to the face looming above him.

"Mr. Sturdley," the brown-haired giant responded. "Here, let me take that. It will make it easier to follow me."

As Maurice relieved Harry of the food and drink, the unshaven pretzel vendor goggled. "You a frienda that guy's?"

"More like a business associate," Sturdley said.

"Big business, I guess," the man said, laughing boisterously.

"From your lips . . ." Harry muttered, setting off into the park, leaving behind two relieved cops but still pursued by part of the crowd.

He'd forgotten how nice Central Park could be in early spring, before the crowds had trampled the life out of the lawns. The scent of new grass and leaves filled the air, with only the occasional whiff of horse manure from the carriages drawn up along the southern end of the park.

With the troop following them, however, Sturdley wondered how long the young grass would survive. The people in the park, enjoying the sunny afternoon, added to the multitude. Strollers, alfresco lunchers, and the usual street people trailed after them as Maurice led the way deeper into the park. The giant set a pace that quickly winded Harry, but it did keep the crowd behind them.

Lawns gave way to a consciously picturesque section, where clumps of schist, the rocky backbone of Manhattan, thrust up through the topsoil. They headed toward the northern end of the pond, which stretched like a moat between the park proper and Fifty-ninth Street. A rocky promontory thrust out into the water, and Maurice boosted Harry up a fairly steep hillside of bare stone. The followers were balked—no paths led this way.

Atop the hill, a copse of trees hid them from view. Maurice laid the food down on a large, squarish boulder just about table size for a pair of giants.

Through the trees, Sturdley discerned Robert standing on the other side of the hill, which sloped more gently down toward open lawn. The giant faced a crowd similar to the one that had pursued them. Unlike Maurice, Robert took a harder line. He faced the gawkers and exploding flashbulbs with his hands on his hips. "Enough," he said in a low rumble. "Now go."

Harry couldn't see the expression on the giant's face, but it must have worked. The crowd quickly dispersed.

Robert joined them by the boulder. Eagerly, the two giants began attacking the sandwiches Sturdley had brought. He'd ordered enough for ten normal-sized people. As he watched the food disappear, he began wondering where he could get sandwiches at a volume discount. Maybe he could make some sort of a deal that could keep the giants fed and bring the restaurant some good publicity, as well.

"You set yourselves up pretty well here," Sturdley said, looking around. "Do you intend to stay?"

"It's away from your traffic, and from prying eyes," Robert said, tossing down a three-inch-thick deli special as if it were a finger sandwich.

"Yeah, pretty much." Sturdley glanced through the overhead canopy of tree branches toward the towering height of the St. Moritz Hotel. Heads filled almost every window he could see. Some windows were open, with television cameras poking out.

"It's easy to defend—" Maurice began.

"—our privacy," Robert smoothly finished.

"Well, this will make a better rendezvous for your meals," Sturdley said. "You can't get away with clogging traffic forever. Otherwise, the hate squads will begin."

"Why should they hate us, when we'll be doing them a favor?" Maurice asked. He opened a gallon container of potato salad, sniffed at it, then shook his head over the tiny implements provided. Digging in with two fingers, he began scooping the salad up to his mouth.

"They may appreciate the fact that you're out here fighting crime," Sturdley said. "But at dinnertime, there's only one thing on the mind of anyone in a car. That's either getting home, or reaching the restaurant where they're going to be fed. And they're going to hate anyone who gets in their way."

"I've seen how they act in their vehicles," Robert said. "A very short-sighted race, these motorists."

"We're short-sighted in general," Sturdley warned. "Take the newspeople. They loved you when you were men of mystery. They got interested when you stopped those punks. But sooner or later, there's going to be a backlash. That's why we've got to set you up with the people as tightly as possible now, while you're still having a honeymoon with the press."

"And how will we do that?" Robert wanted to know. He dug out a pickle. Sturdley had asked for the largest available, but this thing still looked like a baby gherkin in Robert's fingers as the giant popped it in his mouth.

"You need some kind of crusade," Sturdley said. "I've been thinking all morning about what it should be, and I think I've got it. Guns."

"Guns?" Maurice echoed.

"You've shown that guns don't work on you," Sturdley went on eagerly. "Just how bulletproof are you?"

Robert looked down at him, a pinch of cole slaw stopping halfway to his lips. "Our protection is a wall of thought," the giant began, fumbling for words to explain the phenomenon.

"Like a telekinetic force field," Sturdley picked up.

"I see from your mind you grasp the concept," Robert said. He shook away cole slaw juice from another helping.

"And the kids who were picked up the other night said you could spot them, even in the dark. Is that a mental power, too?"

Robert nodded as he chewed.

"Clairvoyance." Sturdley began to get excited. "Can you see through objects as well? Can you tell how many coins I have in my pocket?"

Robert's eyes narrowed as he directed a piercing glance at Sturdley, swallowing his cole slaw. "Three large silver ones, one single small silver, one copper-colored coin just a little larger."

Sturdley took eighty-six cents out of his pocket. "Incredible," he breathed. "Can you do the same thing looking into a car? or a truck?"

Maurice shrugged. "It would be no problem," he said around two sandwiches crammed into his cheeks.

Harry Sturdley leaned forward eagerly, his elbows resting on the rock table. "Okay, then, here's the deal. You've said this city is afraid of crime. What they're most afraid of, though, is guns. A guy feels there's a chance to survive, man to man. But against a gun, most people feel helpless.

"Now, handguns are hard to get in New York—legally. But there's a thriving underground business, buying pistols in other states where they're legal and smuggling them in here.

"So the thing is, you're not going to target criminals, where the media can create a martyr. You're going to go after illegal guns. If you go after the crooks, there'll have to be trials, they have a chance to get off—and their lawyers will smear you. But if you destroy the guns and just hold the crooks for the cops, no matter what happens at the trial, you're Heroes."

"I've heard of these trials." Robert dipped a finger into a bowl of mustard, licked it, and grimaced.

"Who told you about that?" Sturdley demanded.

"There are many who live in this park," Robert replied, using four napkins to clean off his mustardy digit.

Sturdley nodded. "Homeless people. We should provide for them better, but it's hard." He wondered how Robert got the park dwellers to talk to him, then pushed the thought away. There were more important things to discuss.

"Your plan should be to announce what you're going to do. Let the public know what to expect. Maybe we should set up a press conference—"

Robert seemed to be listening intently, then he stared off into the distance. "There are newsgatherers coming here now."

It was inevitable, Sturdley realized. The networks were probably watching from a room in the St. Moritz. When they saw that the giants had company. . . . Harry sighed. He'd hoped to have the giants better prepared, dressed for the occasion in appropriate costumes. Well, they'd have to do the best they could with what they had.

"Listen," he said, "here's what I think we should tell them."

Several camera crews were setting up on the lawn facing the gentler slope of the promontory while Sturdley explained his plan. The foremost crew came from *First News,* with Leslie Ann Nasotrudere in the lead. When she saw Sturdley, a change came over her Barbie Doll features rather like the expression of a lioness scenting fresh meat.

"Mr. Sturdley," she said, aiming herself at Harry. "I thought you said that the Fantasy Factory had no connection with the giants. What, then, are you doing here?" She swung the microphone in Sturdley's direction.

"At the time we spoke, I had no idea who these people were," Sturdley replied, "although I suspected they were heroes. That's what they are indeed, and that's why they wanted to consult me."

"Could you give some details regarding this consultation?" the newswoman pressed.

"I'll leave that up to Robert," Sturdley said, edging away.

Robert rose on the hilltop, the afternoon sun making love to the rippling muscles displayed above his clout. News cameras drank in the vision of his frame. "I wish to send a message to the people of this city," Robert said. "My companion and I have become aware of the fear that grips the citizens' hearts. The fear of crime. We now declare our new home to be a protected city. Let this be a public warning to any who seek to use the tools of terror against this town."

In the firestorm of questions that followed, Robert went on to identify the "tools of terror" as illegal guns. Inwardly, Harry Sturdley rubbed his hands in triumph. The crusade had begun.

Blood was tired by the time he brought the van up to the Holland Tunnel. The drive from down south had been long and boring—worse, because of the strain of keeping to the legal speed limit all the way up. But highway patrol types could be hard-nosed, and he didn't want any cops seeing the load he was carrying. So Blood had spent the entire trip to New York in the right-hand lane.

He was almost dozing through the clogged traffic at the tunnel. Soon enough, though, he'd be crossing Manhattan and taking his load into Brooklyn. In some neighborhoods there, a gun was almost worth its weight in platinum. And everybody knew Blood had the best merchandise.

Now they were chugging their way through the tunnel itself. Blood always had a bad feeling about that, the walls closing in as their progress slowed down. Tonight, the crush of cars and trucks seemed worse than usual.

There, now, he could see the evening sky. The stream of traffic would break up, he'd be able to make some time . . .

Traffic stopped dead as a huge figure stepped into the flow. The dark-haired giant headed straight for Blood's van. "You have guns in there," the big guy boomed.

That was all Blood needed to hear. "Lonnie!" he yelled to his partner in the back of the van. His hand went to the Uzi he kept tucked under his right thigh.

The giant was almost on him by the time Blood got the door open. Aiming vaguely for the massive middle above him, Blood let off a burst.

Six bullets traveling at 1,250 feet per second impacted Maurice's aura. They didn't penetrate, but the force of the shots did spin him halfway around.

Blood was almost behind the wheel again before he realized the giant wasn't falling, just stumbling back a little. He leaned out the door again. "Yo, Lonnie, man, I think we both better shoot this muthaf—"

The giant was coming at him again, anger written all over his face. Blood let go another burst, but the huge figure had braced himself. The snarl of two Uzis filled the tunnel plaza, drowning the cries and screams rising in the air.

"Go for the head, man! Maybe we can get an eye or something!"

The firing behind Blood suddenly ceased. Had Lonnie wasted his clip already? Blood glanced back to find his partner already in the grip of one of the giant monstrosities. He ripped the gun from Lonnie as if he were taking it from a baby.

Then huge fingers were sinking into Blood's arms. He writhed as he was yanked up into the air, trying to bring his gun to bear on the giant's face. Maybe up close like this . . .

But another hand came down to smother the Uzi, twisting it away from Blood. The gun clattered to the ground. Blood clenched his fists, trying to pound on the fingers that held him prisoner. Not a good idea, he suddenly realized. The drop would be like falling out of a second-floor window.

His captor didn't hit him. The giant just held tight and shook Blood's body. It probably didn't seem like much to the big guy, but for Blood, it felt like being flung around the world. His eyes couldn't focus, and his breath came in panting gasps.

Helpless, he dangled in the giant's grasp. The blond guy had put Lonnie down on the side of the road. If Lonnie felt the way Blood did, he wouldn't be going anywhere fast.

The blond giant approached the van, braced himself, then picked up the vehicle. Blood remembered how one of the kids in his neighborhood had gotten a kiddie-car for Christmas; a fire engine maybe three, four feet long. For kicks, Blood had yanked the kid out of the car, picked it up, and thrown it into the middle of Flatbush Avenue.

That's what this big blond guy was doing now— wrestling the van around like it was a kid's toy. He brought it to the side of the road where Blood was held captive. Blood noticed the back door was open where

Lonnie had gotten out. The titan upended the van, shaking out its cargo.

"Illegal guns," the big guy declared, his deep rumble of a voice echoing in the tunnel place. "There is no place for them in this city."

He began picking up Blood's merchandise, crushing the guns in his hands.

Blood began cursing the giant, but his voice was all he could use. He still dangled in the other titan's arms.

Wait a second. His belly gun!

Blood twisted his right arm to the waistband of his pants. He had a little pistol tucked in there, just a .32 caliber. But maybe with the element of surprise, it might be enough to get him free.

He swung around, bringing the gun up toward the dark-haired giant's face. The huge features were a picture of almost comical astonishment as Blood fired the pistol at point-blank range.

For a second, he was falling free as the giant put both hands to his eyes. Then the huge creature snatched out with his right hand. The grip closed cruelly on Blood's arm. Bones grated in his shoulder.

"Yo! Hey! Watch out! My arm!"

The gun fell from nerveless fingers to clatter on the pavement below.

Blood heard sirens and suddenly found himself bathed in glaring light. Through tears of pain, he looked down to see a TV news crew filming him. Using his free arm, he put a hand over his face.

That's that you were supposed to do when the cameras were on you.

CHAPTER 8

Harry Sturdley returned to his Upper East Side apartment with a throbbing headache behind his eyes. He should have been celebrating the greatest negotiating triumph of his life, the dawn of a new age—real, live superheroes!

Instead, he was sitting in an armchair, a cup of tea in his hands. The deal couldn't be clinched, because that nitwit John Cameron was nowhere to be found. Peg had called to give him the bad news, and he had to admit he hadn't been very helpful. "I want the three of you to keep looking until you find him!"

Good management, Sturdley, he reproved himself. He was on edge about stringing the giants along until the kid turned up. For some strange reason, it reminded Sturdley of a show he'd put on while he was still in grammar school. His act was to juggle the Indian clubs, and he'd been standing out on the stage in his underwear, spinning the things around while someone played the piano.

The problem was, the next act, the boy soprano, had

disappeared. Sturdley had to continue juggling frantically, keeping two clubs in the air for what felt like forever. He remembered now, the music was "The Flight of the Bumblebee," and it seemed to get faster and faster . . .

Sturdley was jarred out of his thoughts by the strident ringing of the telephone. His wife Myra answered, then turned to him, a frown on her delicate features. "It's a newsman, calling from One Police Plaza. Your giants are down there."

Sturdley leapt from his easy chair and grabbed the phone. "Who is this?"

"Ted Snopes, International Cable Universal Network," the voice on the other end replied. "Are you aware that the giants known as Robert and Maurice have been taken into custody?"

"On what charge?"

"Does that mean you're ignorant of their actions this evening?"

"It means I'd like to know why two crime-fighters have been taken to the hoosegow." Sturdley clamped his lips to keep from saying anything potentially disastrous over the phone. He'd only been talking to this Snopes character for a few seconds, and already he had a bellyful of his superior attitude. The guy sounded like he was interviewing him . . . uh-oh.

"Hey, Snopes, you recording this?"

"Ah—" Snopes replied, caught off-guard.

"Because this is strictly off the record. You want to talk to me, I'll be down there in half an hour. Now what's the story with these charges?"

"It's very confused." For a second, Snopes sounded

almost human. "There are charges and counter-charges flying back and forth."

"Well, I'll be setting off to get to the bottom of it all—right now. See you later, Snopes." Sturdley replaced the receiver, then started paging through his personal directory. "McManus, McManus. Myra, don't we have Frank McManus' home phone?"

"I'll bet it's on my holiday list," she said, going over to her huge antique desk. Removing a bound collection of cards from one of the pigeonholes, she riffled through them. "Yes, here it is. He's a little farther uptown than we are—a Monument number."

It had been a good twenty years since New York Telephone had turned the letter exchanges into numbers, but Myra still kept them.

Sturdley took the card. Frank McManus answered on the second ring. Sturdley detected loud background noise. It sounded like a fight. "Frank? What's going on?"

McManus sounded a little embarrassed. "I'm reviewing some tapes made by one of our potential licensers—the people who are up for the *Sensational Six* series."

"Does it look as bad as it sounds?"

"Harry, the audio is the good part."

"That's not why I called you." Sturdley abruptly changed gears. "Meet me here at the house. We've got to go downtown and bail some people out"

"Harry?" McManus sounded dumbfounded over the phone. "I'm a corporate lawyer. I do contracts, licensing. I'll be glad to help, but if someone you know is in trouble, they need a criminal lawyer."

"Frank, this *is* corporate business—the biggest license we've ever gotten. If you don't think we can handle it, round up the best criminal guy you know and meet me here ASAP."

McManus picked up Harry as soon as a cab could get him there. They headed down Fifth Avenue. "Ira Orreck and I were in law school together. We're going to his office, it's on the way to the station. Luckily I caught him there, working on a case."

"Orreck? Didn't he defend the Mafia don and a couple of sleazy congressmen?"

Frank McManus nodded. "That's right. No matter how big the case, he won't be overwhelmed by it."

Sturdley permitted himself a smile. "I wouldn't bet on that."

Ira Orreck's leather executive chair was even bigger than the one Sturdley had inherited in his office. Orreck himself was a big, bulky man with a bald head—a Howard Chaykin-esque authority figure. After listening to the case at hand, he sat with his fingers steepled together, his eyes large and a little glazed.

"You're asking me to defend a pair of twenty-foot-tall would-be superheroes?" he finally said when he got his voice back.

"That's it," Sturdley admitted cheerfully. "I'm sure you've seen them on TV already." He leaned forward. "Think of the publicity."

Orreck had already done that. "I don't come cheap."

"My company will handle the fees. But we need somebody down there now to cover them."

The lawyer rose, rolling down his sleeves in preparation for all the TV cameras. "I can do that," he said.

Forty-five minutes later, Robert and Maurice stood outside police headquarters, free giants. Actually, even for their brief incarceration, they had stood outside the headquarters building—there was no room for them in the holding cells.

The glare of camera lights washed over them, especially the three smaller figures at the giants' feet.

"Mr. Orreck," Ted Snopes from ICU called out, "Mr. Frederick Hardiman accuses the giant Maurice of attacking him and manhandling him, resulting in a dislocated shoulder." Snopes shoved his microphone in Orreck's direction.

"What Mr. Hardiman, whose street name, by the way, is Blood, failed to mention was that the alleged 'manhandling' took place after he had discharged a pistol into Maurice' face. The shoulder was dislocated when Maurice caught him while preventing a ten-foot fall. Would it have been better to let the man fall on his head?"

Sturdley hid a smile behind a grave exterior. Orreck was his kind of lawyer, ready to try the case in the media.

"Didn't Mr. Hardiman fall that distance because the giant was holding him up so high?" Leslie Ann Nasotrudere said as she pushed to the front of the news pack. Her hair was elaborately styled, and she was wearing more makeup than usual. Her *First News* blazer was buttoned over a long gown. Apparently, she had cut short some sort of date to cover this story. Equally obvious was the fact that she'd decided the time had come for the backlash.

Concern for "the little guy" was written all over her face as she thrust her microphone at Orreck.

"He was up that high to keep him away from the Uzi

submachine gun he'd been firing, not to mention the truckload of guns he was trying to bring into the city."

"Your so-called heroes stopped the van at the mouth of the Holland Tunnel. Isn't that illegal search and seizure?" Nasotrudere pressed.

"The Heroes have senses beyond those possessed by the rest of us," Orreck said. "One of those is the ability to see, as it were, through the walls of the van. For them, the guns were in plain sight. Does that constitute an illegal search? We'll probably have to leave that determination up to the Supreme Court."

The newswoman's doll-like face changed to incredulity. "Would you have us believe that these creatures can see around corners and into trucks?"

"They demonstrated it to the satisfaction of the police," Sturdley said.

"How did they manage to do that?" Nasotrudere asked with dramatic incredulity.

"They identified the contents of sealed boxes correctly and, for want of a better word, 'saw' the occupants of a windowless room from outside the building," Orreck said.

"And a national TV audience once 'saw' a magician make the Statue of Liberty disappear," Nasotrudere scoffed.

A mutter came from the other media people. Debunking was always big news.

Sturdley stiffened. They were looking at big-time backlash here, unless they did something pretty damned quick.

"Perhaps you'd like to see a demonstration," Sturdley spoke up.

Orreck gave him a look that would have frozen argon, then apparently realized it was their best available tactic. "Would that help convince you, Leslie Ann?"

She reached for her handbag, which was being held by one of her crew people. "If they can find something hidden on my person—something out of the ordinary. It would hardly be impressive to 'find' that I have a watch, for instance, or a red pen in my bag."

Robert was already scanning the newswoman with that intense, piercing gaze. He leaned forward to whisper to Harry Sturdley.

A slow, evil smile curved Happy Harry's lips. "Ms. Nasotrudere, Robert has already detected something unique on your person, something none of the other newspeople has."

Every eye and camera turned to Sturdley.

"From the description Robert has given me, you've got a letter in your handbag—a letter with the logo of a rival network."

Caught in the act of opening her handbag, Leslie Ann Nasotrudere jerked as if Sturdley had just goosed her. The bag dropped from her hands, hitting the sidewalk and spilling its contents.

Evil joy glittered in the eyes of Ted Snopes as he picked up a piece of paper with a nationally known red and blue logo. "This appears to be a follow-up letter from the producer of the network's national news— after your lunch with him. It would seem you're in the midst of negotiations not merely to jump networks but to leave local newscasting." Waving the letter in one hand, he aimed his mike at the newswoman with the other. "Do you have any comment, Leslie Ann?"

"When were you going to let your station know?" another reporter chimed in.

"Would you be staying in New York, or moving to another city?" another newsie called.

For the first time in front of a camera, Leslie Ann Nasotrudere's plastic facade cracked. She turned bright red, and when she tried to speak, sounds like "Ommma-homma" came out.

The cameras turned from Sturdley to zero in on the hapless newswoman. Rampaging giants were now old hat. An ace newswoman pulling a Letterman was now the hot story.

Sturdley turned away to hide a grin as the pack of newshounds now turned on one of their own.

The giants stared down, baffled at the antics of the Lessers around their feet.

Ira Orreck, however, frowned. "You made us a powerful enemy tonight, Sturdley."

Happy Harry shrugged. "She was an enemy already," he pointed out to the lawyer. "Right now, she's suffered a powerful shutdown. Or at least a temporary diversion, as she deals with her so-called colleagues."

The news crews swirled around Leslie Ann Nasotrudere. Sturdley caught a glimpse of her now pale face as she struggled to escape.

She saw him and darted a poisonous glance at him.

Yes, Sturdley thought, he had made an enemy.

What had happened to the old-style news people? he lamented. In the days of his youth, there was no *media*, only newspapers. And newspapermen came from the people—roughneck, hard-drinking, sort of urban good old boys. Maybe it was bad tactics, but it had felt damn good to take Nasotrudere down a peg tonight. She'd be too busy trying to rescue her network deal to make any trouble. That is, if she weren't exiled to news reading out in the boonies.

Tomorrow, though . . .

"I guess we'll have to set up a press conference to demonstrate the heroes' powers," Sturdley said. "In, ah, less circus-like circumstances."

He glanced up at the two figures towering over him. "Well, come on, guys, you're free. Did they treat you all right?"

From above came a hollow rumble, a borborygmal sound of hunger.

"No dinner," Maurice said in some embarrassment.

Sturdley whispered to Orreck, "I almost wish the cops *had* kept them. Do you know how much these bastards can eat?"

CHAPTER 9

Arriving home, Sturdley was almost afraid to check the media reaction on the late-night news.

Unsurprisingly, *First News* had very little to say about giants or the revelations they had to make, but the other networks all had their version of the "Gargantua Follies," as one commentator called it. Clips of the red-faced Leslie Ann Nasotrudere being asked whether she'd be leaving town appeared on every show.

The response to the gun raid was surprisingly positive, especially the "man-in-the-street" interviews with rush-hour commuters featured on the early-morning news shows the next day. New Yorkers definitely liked the idea of someone destroying illegal guns, even if they suspected the gun smugglers themselves would get off on technicalities.

There was also an interesting side note: a would-be mugger found gibbering in the middle of Central Park. Pieces of a pistol—crushed pretty fine—were found strewn around him, not to mention giant, four-inch-deep footprints.

"The boys had a busy night," Sturdley said, but he felt a niggling doubt burrowing under his contentment. Harry knew his priorities: get the giants under contract, into uniforms, and onto the pages of his comic books. The problem was that Robert had his own agenda: bringing in more of his people . . . through the agency of John Cameron. Try as he might, Sturdley could not manage to get his mind around the fact that the kid was central to the whole deal. He'd written dozens of plots where characters went from zeros to heroes—but *John Cameron*, for chrissake? Sturdley was haunted with the fear the whole deal would turn out to be some sort of gigantic prank.

He was rising to turn off the television when his attention was caught by one of those last-minute newsbits that are supposed to be cute. It was a picture of Robert beside—horrors!—a sketch of Ram-Man, Dynasty Comics' lead hero. The giant wore his usual skimpy diaper-like loin covering. In the drawing, Ram-man, "The Black-sheep Avenger," was togged out in the usual midnight-blue long underwear, cowl with curving horns, and heavy cape.

The perky blond anchorwoman aimed a come-hither grin at the camera. "Although comics have been criticized for revealing too much anatomy on superhero-ines, the opposite seems to be true of our real-life Heroes. They wear a lot less than most of their four-color counterparts. There's no uniform on that Greek-god bod, and a lot of our female viewers are saying it would be a shame to cover it with a cape."

Obligatory chuckles came from the station crew. "And how do you feel about that, Kara-Jean?" the male anchor asked, a smirk on his chiseled features.

"At his size, I think Robert may just be too much of a good thing," Kara-Jean responded with her sexy smile.

On his way down to the office, Happy Harry had the cab stop at Central Park. Then he walked to the promontory over the pond, the new breakfast rendezvous spot. Robert and Maurice sat quietly by the rock table, although the Fantasy Factory gofer with their food wouldn't be along for another half-hour.

"Checking to make sure we get fed?" Robert asked with a smile.

"I wanted to see if you were having gawker problems," Sturdley said.

The giant shrugged. "It's a bit too early yet. What I pick up from the minds of the passersby is the need to get to work. Some stop on the sidewalk and peer, but we're too far way—and hidden in these trees."

"Nobody's bothered you?"

Maurice grinned. "Some come climbing up, but Robert takes care of them."

The blond giant demonstrated his technique, looming over Harry, then bending low to bring his huge, scowling face closer. "I think you've come too close," he said in a deep rumbling voice.

"After that, they keep their distance," Maurice said.

Sturdley nodded. "I have another question for you. Are those jock-strap things you wear the usual clothes for people on your world?"

Robert looked down with surprise at his clout. "The Less—that is, people like you, seem to feel the weather more than we do. They wear a variety of coverings. For ourselves, we see little need."

"What about rain?"

Maurice shrugged. "Our auras deflect it."

"Perhaps it also helps with the cold," Robert added. "I've heard that discussed."

"Don't you need clothes for safety?" Sturdley pressed.

That only got him baffled looks. "Safety from what?" Maurice asked.

"I don't know. Animals, people . . ."

"Animals on our world are more of a size to endanger you than us," Robert said.

"And your people can't hurt us," Maurice chimed in.

"But what about threats from other people your size?" Sturdley asked.

Looks like I hit a nerve, he thought, not enjoying the glances he was getting.

"Differences between our people are settled personally," Robert said in a flat voice. He obviously didn't want to say more.

"Hey, I'm sorry if I offended you," Sturdley said, his shirt getting sticky as he realized he may have unintentionally jeopardized the deal. "I just wanted to know why you wear those little things."

Maurice reached down to his clout and jiggled it slightly. "We wouldn't," he finally said, "except for the low-hanging branches."

A deflated Harry Sturdley set off to find himself a cab downtown.

"I've got to find out more about wherever they used to live," he muttered.

Leslie Ann Nasotrudere's prime-time features were a mask of fury as she glared at the phone. "What do you mean, I'm not coming in today?" she demanded of her news director.

"It comes from network—from the Veep for News," her boss responded in a tone just as nasty—payback for all the abuse he'd had to take from his star reporter. "The official word is that you're sick. Unofficially, you are not to make yourself available for interviews from representatives of other networks. At least, not as long as you're working for *First News.*"

A chill ran down Leslie Ann's back. Her bosses were playing hardball. It was one thing to break a contract and move to another network, but if she got fired, she'd lose cachet. Would another network want damaged goods?

And face it, she told herself, *you got damaged pretty bad on the air last night.*

"All right," she said through tight lips. "I'm home sick today."

"Just disconnect your phone. The network will handle all press inquiries," she was told.

"But I've got stuff scheduled today," Leslie Ann said. "There's the interview with the Guardian Angels for my piece on the rise of vigilantism, and the President is coming to town—"

"The first item is canceled for the time being, and the other will be covered by Chuck Flamboy."

Small wrinkled appeared on Leslie Ann's forehead at hearing that the First News anchor was going into the field to do her stories. Finally, it was sinking in that her whole career was in danger.

"We'll be sending an appropriate statement for release to the press," the news director said. "If things blow over by tomorrow, I've got a couple of things in the South Bronx I'd like you to look into. Talk to you soon."

Leslie Ann made every effort to sound agreeable as she hung up the phone. The South Bronx—the Siberia of local newscasting. The only times that neighborhood appeared on the screen was quadrennially, when presidential candidates stopped by. Sometimes, if there was a gruesome enough murder, the area got a few minutes of airtime. Doing a non-murder piece on the South Bronx meant having to work the whole earnest-examination-of-a-depressed-neighborhood shtick. That made for dull TV news. And it wouldn't help her standing any, right now.

"*Damn* Sturdley!" she said through her teeth. She didn't know how he knew about that letter, unless his pet freaks actually did do magic tricks.

Leslie Ann Nasotrudere did know one thing. She would make this so-called comic book king pay for what he'd done to her. He'd pay big-time.

A glum-faced trio sat around Peg Faber's desk.

"There's not a picture of him around *anywhere*?" Peg asked.

"Let's face it, they don't take any at personnel," Elvio Vital said. "I don't think we have a personnel, do we?"

"But there's always parties, and blurbs in the books," Peg said. "Wait a second! We had a photographer come in at the last Christmas bash. He took a group shot of everybody."

"Everybody but John Cameron," Marty Burke said in disgust, holding up a slightly crumpled photo. "I happened to remember that, too."

Peg shook her head. "I've heard of people being camera-shy, but this is ridiculous. We'll have to ask everybody in the office, just to make sure."

Sometime later, they were back at Peg's desk.

"Nobody?" she moaned. 'We can't go searching for him if we don't have a picture." Peg looked nervously down the hallway. Any minute now, Harry Sturdley would come walking up, demanding to know what they were doing to find John Cameron. They had to have something to show him.

She turned decisively to Marty Burke. "You're an artist. Draw a picture of his face."

Burke stared at her as if she'd grown an extra eye. "What?"

"Draw a sketch of John's face," Peg repeated, keeping each word down to one syllable. "Get it now?"

Marty Burke shook his head. "That's not what I do."

"What are you talking about? You draw for a living! I don't want to tell Harry that you refused to help, but when he comes in—"

Burke's pose of artistic hauteur cracked. "I don't draw things out of my head," he confessed in annoyance. "I use reference. Photo reference. If we had a picture of the kid, I could draw him."

Peg's fingers became claws on her desk top. "If we had a picture of John, we wouldn't need you to draw him!"

When Sturdley finally came in to his office, he found Elvio Vital sitting by Peg's desk, a portable sketchboard in his lap.

"Don't tell me *you're* drawing her into one of your books now, too," Sturdley said.

Peg's red curls were almost touching Elvio's tousled locks as she peered over the board. "I think his nose is a little wider."

Elvio held up the board, showing Sturdley a surprisingly realistic and accurate representation of John Cameron.

"Gah!" Sturdley said. "Don't do that to me!"

Then he took another look at Cameron à la Elvio. "I didn't know you could draw like that," he said, looking at the carefully shaded pencil sketch.

"I didn't always do my scribbly little funny people, you know," Elvio responded. "I drew other things before them."

"He gave me a lovely painting for Christmas," Peg said.

That was something else Sturdley hadn't known— not that Elvio could paint, but that he gave Peg one of his pictures. Apparently, even Elvio wasn't impervious to Peg's pert, redheaded charms.

"About this," Harry said, tapping the picture on the board. "You haven't quite captured him yet. Make him look dopier."

"We're going to hit all the comic shops in town," Peg said. "Maybe he's got friends out there. I've already asked everybody here in the offices. The last anyone saw John was right after he delivered the coffee to your meeting."

"Have you called the cops yet?" Sturdley asked.

Peg's face went dead pale.

"He's been gone long enough to be considered a

missing person. That way, you won't have to be checking the jails, hospitals—"

"Or morgues," she said in a shaky voice.

"Hey, I'm just trying to help you," Sturdley quickly said.

"I was thinking about it anyway," Peg admitted. "He left that place in Astoria without taking his comic collection along. I can't imagine him leaving it behind voluntarily."

"You're right," Elvio agreed. "That doesn't sound like the John we know."

"Tell Frank McManus that I want him to take care of talking to the cops," Sturdley said. "Maybe he's got a useful contact there."

Stepping into his office, Sturdley frowned. He'd left his assistant tied up with this search for Cameron, not to mention his prime humor artist and Mr. Fan Favorite. If this kept up, he'd have to do something about their books. Elvio, the fastest pen in New York, probably wouldn't have a problem with lost time. Besides, *The Electrocutioner* was a humor book, without a continuing plot.

Replacing Burke could be more of a problem, since *Mr. Pain* was in the middle of a story arc. They'd just have to go with a fill-in story, as well as a fill-in artist. Fabian Thibault had done the title before Burke took over. Maybe he had a leftover story in the trunk. A grim smile lit Sturdley's face. Marty the Genius would raise holy hell over this, but he wouldn't have much choice. Besides being late on *Latter-Day Breed,* he was also supposed to be working on *The Death of the Glamazon.* It would be fun to see him caught on the horns of a dilemma.

Sturdley picked up his phone and dialed Gunnar's extension. He could work without Peg, maybe get a gofer to hold down her desk while she was out. He'd done it before, between assistants.

"Bob," he said, as the phone was answered, "we've got to get some backup going for Burke's books. Maybe Elvio's, too. I don't know how long this search is going to take. No, I gave them the job, and they're going to take care of it. If they need more troops, give them first priority on the gofers—except for me. Once you get that straightened out, I want you to come in here with some artists—our best costume design people. We've got to dress up Robert and Maurice."

He hung up, then began dialing Frank McManus' number.

Gunnar and the troops arrived just as Harry was finishing with the lawyer.

"All right, Harry," McManus sighed over the line. "I'll find *somebody* with clout."

"Maybe your friend Orreck can help," Sturdley suggested. "We'll be paying him enough as it is."

Hanging up the phone, he turned to the people trooping through his doorway. With Gunnar were two young artists, Kyle Everard and Zeb Grantfield.

Good choices, Sturdley thought. Everard routinely created new characters for the *Schizodroid* title, since the hero was a being with multiple personality, each with its own superpower. And because Grantfield drew all of his faces alike, he was always designing new costumes so that readers could identify the characters in his book. And, both Lawson and Grantfield knew how to draw costumes *tight*.

"How's *Jumboy* coming along?" Sturdley asked

Grantfield. It wouldn't hurt to remind the artist that the boss was keeping an eye on him.

"That Nagel guy sure can lay out a page," Grantfield said. "We got a good day's work done."

"Good, because I've got another project for you," Sturdley said. "I want you two to start designing costumes for twenty-foot-tall people."

"You mean for-real costumes? Like for the giants?" Lawson said.

"Exactly." Sturdley nodded. "They've established themselves as crime-fighters, and we're going to be doing at least one book about them. So they've got to have costumes—unless we're going to call it *The Adventures of Nakedman*."

Everard shrugged. "Well, ya know, some of the independents have been having success with that X-rated stuff—"

He subsided under angry glares from both Gunnar and Sturdley.

"Just remember one thing," Sturdley pointed out. "Your designs will have to be turned into real clothes. Bear that in mind as you're drawing."

"Yeah," Everard said with a sigh.

"That a problem?" Sturdley asked.

The artist smiled. "It's a lot easier to go for *tight* when you can paint the clothes on."

Sturdley dismissed the artists but beckoned Gunnar to stay.

"Well, there's half the project." Happy Harry put a hand to his eyes. That headache was setting in again.

"Getting the costumes actually made will be the other half," Gunnar said.

Sturdley smiled. "I used to have some school friends in the rag trade," he said. "Maybe they can help me find someone who can give me a nice price on a few dozen yards of Spandex."

CHAPTER 10

Peg Faber was not happy to be back in Astoria, even though this time she'd prepared herself in advance with petty cash for the cabfare, but the police were now going over the apartment where John Cameron had disappeared, and she wanted to be there.

"This is a waste of time," Marty Burke complained before they even got out of the cab. Three police cars were parked in front of the brick apartment building. One officer stood on guard in the courtyard.

"I don't know what Mr. McManus said, but he certainly got quick service," Peg said.

"Yeah, it's impressive, but it's guarding the stable after the horse is gone." Burke went to push by the cop, only to get a beefy hand in his chest.

"State your business, please," the officer said.

From the tone of his voice, the "please" was just a turn of phrase.

"We're from the Fantasy Factory, where John Cameron worked. Works," Peg quickly corrected herself. "I'm Peg Faber, assistant to the publisher, this is

Elvio Vital, and the gentleman with you is Marty Burke."

The cop drew himself up, then said, "*The* Marty Burke? No foolin'. So when is this *Latter-Day Breed* project finally coming out?"

Peg shook her head as Burke blossomed into a celebrity. Comics fans—you never knew where you were going to bump into them. They got the VIP treatment all the way up to Apartment 4-B, especially after Burke promised the cop on guard an autographed copy of the premier issue of *Latter-Day Breed* when it finally came out.

Once inside, they found the immigrant family who had rented the room to John huddled in the front hallway. Low moans in what they still presumed was Carpathian came from the grandmotherly woman. Beside her, trying to calm her down, was a tall, stooped man with a dark complexion and fierce black moustache. The rest of him didn't look fierce, only tired. There was also a younger woman, looking prematurely old and scared to death.

Finally, there was a little boy, maybe four years old, who looked thrilled to have police in the apartment. Whenever a cop went by, he raised a finger and went "Bang-bang!"

When the old woman saw them, she raised a commotion. The only word Peg recognized was "Draghi," which she recalled was the man's name. Their escort turned them over to a police sergeant, who was attempting to question the family.

"You're the people who discovered the disappearance?" he asked, looking up from a notebook.

The elderly woman nodded her head vehemently. "They come. But he gone. Gone already!"

"No get rent," the man named Draghi said. "He go in, I knock on door, no answer. Knock harder. I know he in there. So I fix. I wait, watch all night, so he no sneak out."

"Couldn't you have fallen asleep?" the sergeant suggested.

"Work nights. That one of my night off," Draghi replied.

"Couldn't you have fallen asleep anyway?" the police officer pressed.

"I fix. Tie string from door to here." Draghi pointed to his ankle. "Sit there." He indicated a straight wooden chair set at an angle to John Cameron's door. Peg had suspected that's where the grandmother had stationed herself, as well.

"Door open, string pull. I wake up."

The cop stared in bafflement from the doorknob to the chair. That would have been a very effective wake-up device. "Did he know you were out there?"

Draghi shook his head vigorously. "Want to catch him when he sneak."

The door was splintered now, thanks to Elvio's demonstration of his martial arts technique. But it had been a solid barrier. There was no peephole, no way John could have seen Draghi waiting.

"Well, he got out that door somehow," the cop said, a little steamed. "There's no other way. That window is stuck solid." He turned to the elderly woman. "When you took over, did you go away at any time?"

The woman looked scared under her babushka, but she shook her head. "Not even go bathroom."

"We do notting to him," the younger woman suddenly spoke up in a trembling voice.

Peg suddenly realized why she was nervous. The woman was afraid the police were about to charge them with murder or something.

The older woman went to the doorway of the room, peering in. Police officers filled the airless little space. The bed was up, the comic boxes had been shifted around. There was no place to hide a body.

"He go in," the woman insisted. "Then, poof! Gone!"

The police sergeant questioned Sturdley's searchers, asking what they had done and what they had seen. Then he shrugged. "I don't get this one," he admitted, "but we're making the rounds of the hospitals and such. Did he have any close friends at work?"

"Not really close," Peg admitted. "We were asking around ourselves." She wished she hadn't been given this job. It was like trying to pin down a phantom.

Before heading back to Manhattan, they checked out the local comics shop. The owner was rude, didn't recognize John's picture and, worst of all in Burke's eyes, didn't recognize him as the famous Marty Burke.

They had better luck in Manhattan. There, Peg had to admit, the name Burke meant something, opening doors and loosening tongues. Store owners were eager to help in the hopes of getting some of their stock autographed.

Most of them managed to annoy Burke, however, by asking when the long-delayed *Latter-Day Breed* was coming out.

They finally hit paydirt on Twenty-third Street. The owner of the comics shop in the old hotel glanced over his heavy, black-framed glasses at Elvio's sketch. "Sure I know him," he said. "That's John Cameron."

The man leaned forward for a better look, handing off the carton of comics he was carrying to Marty Burke. Although he was taller and broader, the stocky artist staggered under the load.

Taking the sketch in his hand, the store owner explained that John often bought comics there, since they had a policy of selling comics to professionals.

"Of course, John wasn't a professional—yet," the man said with a smile. "But he had talent. I saw what he did for the day-care center at the Y."

Peg glanced at her companions. They'd definitely check this out later. "When was the last time you saw him?" she asked.

The store owner shrugged. "It's been a few days. He missed buying the last shipment of comics."

With a little prompting, they were able to ascertain that John hadn't been there since before his last appearance at the Fantasy Factory.

"Did he have any friends here?" Peg asked for what felt like the thousand and fifth time.

The owner shook his head. "He was pleasant, a good listener. But he tended to stay to himself. Sometimes he joined in on the shop talk. John was a good kid. Caught a shoplifter in here once."

Peg thanked him, though she didn't like the use of the past tense.

The Y.M.C.A. was across the street and down the block. When Peg asked to see the day-care center, she was led to a large cinder-block room that could have been grim. Maybe it had been once, but now it was brightly painted, the walls decorated with exuberantly executed portraits of comic characters. The artist, they were told, had been John Cameron.

"He's a member here and donated his time," the woman who ran the center told Peg. "We were happy to get clean, fresh-painted walls. But he offered to brighten the place up, and the kids love it."

"Wump! Wump!" A little boy chanted as he danced in front of a picture of the Petulant Lump in an uncharacteristic pose. The diapered hero had a big grin on his face and seemed to be waving to the kids in the hall.

In fact, Peg realized, all the characters on the walls looked cheerful, and a lot more engaging than they did in their various books.

Elvio Vital stood beside the dancing boy, his eyes scanning the wall. "I see he drew the competition's heroes as well," he said, nodding to a gray-clad flying figure with a big orange Z on his chest. The Man of Molybdenum seemed to be good-naturedly buzzing the Lump. The Sensational Six—Jumboy, Hotbreath, Dark Matter, Waterwoman, and the team leader, Dr. Rush—were there, too, in a smiling group portrait. "And there's the Sproing," Elvio went on, pointing to a hero with coiled-steel legs. "But who's this?" He stepped along the wall, stopping to squint at a picture of a helmeted hero in what appeared to be a suit of crimson armor.

"Maybe he's setting up his own comics universe," Burke sneered. "Or he picked up a picture from some grade-Z small press." He turned to Peg. "What do you think, Faber?"

Peg was facing the far wall, staring wide-eyed. "That picture there. Do those guys look familiar?"

The painting showed a forest with a pair of forms

that towered over the trees. One titan was blond, the other dark-haired. The picture was too small to show faces, but both figures wore something between breech-clouts and diapers.

Marty and Elvio stood in silence.

"He couldn't have done that," Burke said, a little hoarse. "That broad at the door said this was painted months ago. How could Cameron have known about them?"

"He couldn't. He had to have made them up. But how . . . ?" An involuntary shiver shook Peg's frame.

Elvio Vital continued to run a speculative eye over the artwork. "You know, the kid really can draw."

"He probably traced it or projected it, something like that," Burke said sourly.

"I wouldn't knock his style so much if I were you, Marty," Elvio said. "Now that I see it in front of me, so big, I realize who he draws like."

"Who?" Burke demanded.

"You," Elvio Vital responded.

Burke turned a light shade of green as he went back to looking at the walls. "It *does* look something like the way I draw. But I haven't done a lot of these figures, so he can't be swiping my work," he admitted.

Peg smiled. That was high praise, if grudgingly, given from Marty Burke. They'd certainly discovered some new sides to the elusive John Cameron. He was a good enough artist to impress two top professionals. He caught shoplifters, and helped a day-care center. She'd never have expected any of that from the kid she knew at the Fantasy Factory.

The smile faded as a chill suddenly crept up Peg's spine. Ever since the giant had come to Harry's office asking for John Cameron, she hadn't been able to believe it was real.

Now it seemed all too real.

And a bit scary, too.

Once upon a time, Times Square had been the mecca for novelty and magic stores. Over the years, however, times, and Times Square, had changed. Now the only novelties available were inflatable ones marked "Adults Only." The magic had gone out of the neighborhood, and with it, the magic stores.

Except for Geltner's.

Sammy Geltner's grandfather had run a magic shop here, and so had his father. But Sammy was the last of the Geltners, and he was no kid anymore. He'd had to adjust to the prevailing conditions, which meant eliminating half the stock space and bringing in arcade games. They attracted a rough crowd, but Sammy had to pay the rent. When he died, the magic would go altogether, and it would be all machines.

That might be sooner than he expected, Sammy thought, looking down the muzzle of the gun pointed at his head.

"Jus' gimme the money and ya don't get hurt." The kid behind the gun was of indeterminate color, race, and accent. He was the kind of mixed-up kid that New York produced so well. And now the gumball machine of fate had just dropped him on Sammy Geltner.

The kid was nervous. Sammy could tell that by the way the gun kept jerking around all over the place. Either this was a first-time job, or the kid was on something.

"The money is mainly in quarters, you know," Sammy said quietly.

"Jus' gimme it!"

Sammy didn't have a choice. He got out a shopping bag, proudly inscribed so long ago with the name "Geltner's Novelties," and began filling it up.

"Tha's 'nuff," the kid suddenly snapped, grabbing hold of the bag and snatching it off the counter. The weight of the quarter rolls was enough to drag his skinny frame off-balance. For a second, the gun flew off-target. If Sammy had been twenty years younger . . .

No. Not even then. Sammy Geltner was no superhero.

The kid stumbled away with the surprisingly heavy bag, opened the door, then turned back, raising the gun, his lips stretching in a mirthless grin.

Time seemed to stretch into eternity as Sammy waited for that twitchy finger to tighten on the trigger.

But then a giant shadow appeared in the doorway, and huge fingers dove down to engulf the gun.

The kid gave a sudden bleat of fear, and the pistol discharged. The enormous fist shook, jerking the thief off-balance and sending him to the floor.

However, the gun stayed in the massive hand. The titanic form outside bent forward, so that Sammy Geltner could now see the giant's chilling blue eyes.

"No more guns!" a deep, rumbling voice growled over the sound of rending metal.

The giant had broken the barrel off the pistol. Now he ground the whole gun up, strewing the pieces over the shivering figure on the floor.

Footsteps came pounding up, and the local beat cop

appeared behind the giant, his gun drawn. "What's going on here?" the officer barked.

"What's going on is that this kid tried to rob me, and this big fella just saved my life," Geltner reported in economical fashion.

The shop owner shuffled to the doorway. "Son," he said, looking up at the blond giant, "you deserve a reward. What can I do for you? You want a meal? A big fella like yourself could always use a meal, I bet. Or maybe some money?"

The blond giant shook his head with a smile. Then he stopped, his eye caught by something in the display window. "Is that a real pack of cards?" he asked.

Sammy Geltner glanced over at the pack of oversized magician's cards in the window—three times normal size, perfect for large audiences.

"Yes, they're real playing cards. A little dusty, maybe, but real. Would you like them?"

Sitting cross-legged on the hilltop boulder that he considered their table, Robert shuffled the cards and began to deal. They looked at their hands, and Maurice said, "I'll take two."

Robert flipped the cards face-down to his companion.

"Dealer takes one." He peeled off a card, looked at it, and felt a mild twinge of triumph. It wasn't often he managed to draw to an inside straight.

Robert hadn't spent the last few days merely patrolling. He'd explored this incredible city, finding many things to wonder over. Standing outside a large building, he'd discovered children inside, learning to read. Carefully probing their minds, he'd picked up the written form of the local language. Since then, wherever he could pick up a scrap of reading matter, he'd devoured it, despite the clumsiness of the size and the fact that all print below headlines rated as small print to his eyes.

Discarded newspapers had taught Robert that the world he'd stumbled into was full of tremendous machines and terrible weapons. He'd learned there were other huge cities besides this one, that the local Master of Masters was called a President, and that he was often assailed by his subjects. There was some sort of council called a Congress, which shared the rulership. He had much to learn, but one thing was certain—this was a world where anything was possible.

But he still hadn't thought to hope for a deck of cards that he could handle. The suits of cards were different, but he and Maurice had quickly adapted them to their native game.

They revealed their cards.

"Gods below!" Maurice swore as Robert once again swept the pot of pebbles to his side of the table.

The players both stopped as they detected a familiar mind at the outskirts of the crowd on the far side of the hill. It had taken some harsh looks from them both, as well as some strong words from Robert, but the Lessers had learned to keep their distance.

Harry Sturdley climbed up an empty slope. "The blond guy is gonna chase you away," one of the tourists in the crowd called after him.

"Do you realize that your little card game is going out live all over creation?" Sturdley demanded when he reached the hilltop.

Robert had learned about television, and even seen

some of his exploits being replayed on videotape in the windows of appliance stores. "They're a gift from a man whose life I saved."

"I know about that," Sturdley growled. "Nice touch. But I'm more concerned about you playing poker in front of the TV cameras." He blinked. "How do you know poker, anyway?"

Robert shrugged. "Some games must be universal," he said. "But I don't understand your reaction. We patrolled, as you said, and we'll patrol again later, after a few more games. What's the problem?"

"The problem is you're gambling," Sturdley said. "That's something frowned on by the comics code."

"Ah—your famous code for fictional heroes," Robert said. "Well, when you tell our stories, just leave out the card games."

"But people will know about them!" Sturdley fumed. "At least when there are cameras around, can't you play something a little more innocuous, like Go Fish?"

"I don't know that game," Robert said. "And from the impression I get from your mind, I don't think I'd like it."

He glanced at the boulder, with its piles of pebbles on either side. "This is merely for pleasure, not the way we used to play the game back home."

Robert glanced over the crowd of onlookers that filled the rolling lawns. "We can't play for the stakes we normally used."

CHAPTER 11

Harry returned to his office in a bad mood. Peg could hear him stomping down the hallway, even though it was carpeted. "I dunno if I want to keep one of our people on the media watch," he was telling Bob Gunnar. "Every report I get just seems to raise my blood pressure."

Peg sat behind her desk, her hands clasped together so tightly her knuckles hurt. She'd have to report to Harry in a couple of minutes to tell him his search team had blown it.

Spread on the desk in front of her were the meager things they knew or had learned about John Cameron: Elvio's drawing, her brief report, notification from the police, and the form he'd filled out when he joined the Fantasy Factory. It wouldn't make much of a file. Stick it under "F"—for failure.

Between herself and the artists, they'd spread a net through the comics scene of New York. The police had covered the real world. Nothing. It seemed that John Cameron was nowhere in New York.

Peg's eyes rested for a second on the application form. *Nowhere in New York . . .*

She snatched up the piece of paper as Harry Sturdley came into view. "Any luck?" he grunted.

"No, but do you have a minute?"

Sturdley gestured toward his office door. "What's the story?"

"We've searched all over New York and haven't found a trace of him."

An unhappy Harry Sturdley sank into the leather executive's chair. "I don't need to hear this," he groaned. "I'm holding this deal together with spit and personality—and I'm running out of both. The giants are beginning to get a little restless."

His expression became more sour. "The guy who delivered lunch to them thinks he saw someone from Decrepit Comics hanging around Maurice. I thought this would be a nice, simple job of rounding up the office nerd. Now it looks like I'll have to bring in the FBI."

"He's not a nerd," Peg said, a little surprised to find herself standing up for the vanished gofer. "He's a darned good artist, has a big heart—"

"And the smallest attention span of any gofer in Fantasy Factory history," Sturdley finished for her. "Stop thinking of him as a mystery man, Peg. There are two mysteries about John Cameron. First, how he manages to impersonate a human being, and second, how long he'll stay alive when I finally get my hands on him," Happy Harry growled.

But Peg shook her head. "There's a lot we don't know about John—like how he spends his time outside of work." She described the pair of giants painted on the wall of the day-care center. "That was done months before Robert and Maurice appeared."

Sturdley scowled. The whole situation—the giants, the deal, and John Cameron—sat in front of him like some cosmic jigsaw puzzle. The only problem was that the pieces were all the same color—and none seemed to fit together. He had no idea what the final product would look like.

"Everything you discover about the kid makes him seem weirder and weirder," Harry said.

"On the contrary I've discovered that John's a bit like me," Peg responded.

Her boss bitterly shook his head. "Don't say such things."

"We've got one similarity," Peg insisted. "Neither of us is a native New Yorker. I just saw it on his application. There's one place we haven't thought to look: his hometown."

Sturdley looked up. "And where is this hometown?" he asked.

"Cameron Corners, West Virginia."

"I should have guessed," Happy Harry muttered. "Some wide spot in the road to nowhere. At least it explains the boy wonder."

Peg looked puzzled.

"Inbreeding," Sturdley said acidly. "In this case, it produced a sport of nature."

"That's not very nice," Peg huffed. "Especially when you need John so badly."

"Just find him for me," Sturdley said. "I'll take care of the sweet-talking."

"Let me check the flight schedules," she said, trying

to regain her dignity. Peg frowned on the way out. What was the matter with her?

She went to her desk and called the company travel agent. It seemed like Cameron Corners wouldn't exactly be on the main travel itinerary. They would have to go to Washington, take a commuter run to Charlotte, then rent a car. It took the travel agent a moment or two even to find Cameron Corners.

When Peg returned to Sturdley's office, her face was a little red.

"So what did you find out about East Cupcake, or wherever it was?" Happy Harry asked.

"They changed the name of the town from Cameron Corners to, uh—"

"I can hardly wait," Sturdley said. "What is it now, Horseapple Acres?"

"Kokomo," Peg admitted.

She kept quiet while Sturdley broke into laughter. "The good news is that if I leave right now, I can be there by evening."

Sturdley shot her a sharp look. "What's this 'I' stuff? You're part of a team. Vital and Burke are going with you."

"To Kokomo?"

He nodded. "You'd better get on the horn to the travel agency and let them know."

"Burke's not going to like it. He's already complaining that he's losing time on *Latter-Day Breed*."

Sturdley smiled. "Yeah."

Then his face got serious. "Peg."

"What's the matter, Harry?"

"Be careful with Elvio."

"What?"

"He gave you a painting. Now you'll be off in South Armpit with him. Don't—"

"Harry, what do you think? I'm a grown-up. And this is a business trip." Peg paused for a moment. "I thought you'd be warning me against Burke."

"I have better faith in your taste. Elvio is a nice guy."

Peg smiled. "You've got a point there. But you don't have to worry about me."

"Good." Sturdley looked down at the papers on his desk. "Now leave me alone. I've got a speech to write for Robert." He grimaced. "I have the horrible feeling that I may be creating a whole new product line for Decrepit Comics."

Peg's face got very serious. "We'll pull it off, Harry." She headed purposefully out of the office.

"Just make sure you've got somebody covering your desk while you're away," Sturdley called after her.

An hour later, Harry's speechwriting was interrupted by the phone. "Somebody get that," he yelled.

"Okay," shouted Eddie Walcott, the young gofer who was subbing for Peg.

A second later, Eddie's voice came over the intercom. "It's a Cousin Louie."

Harry's hand went back to work on his eyes. "Which one?"

"There's more than one?" Eddie said.

The press conference had filled the seats of the skating rink just north of the giants' promontory homestead. Robert stood on the hill crest, ringed by reporters and television cameras.

"Some people have been calling us Heroes," the giant said. "I've read about their hopes, seen their fears. They wonder what we're going to do."

He scanned the crowd around him. "We're going to keep it up. We won't stop until every illegal gun in this city is destroyed. Guns plus criminals equal terror—for the victims, for innocents on the streets caught in cross fire, for the people who fear to leave their homes at night. Our effort is to eliminate the means, to put an end to the terror."

Robert smiled. "Perhaps, if we're successful, police will be able to patrol like—what were they called? The London bobbies."

"You mean no guns?" a reporter asked.

"That is the hope," Robert said.

More questions followed, and Harry Sturdley stood off to the side, looking respectful. Robert was getting quite polished at human relations.

When the newspeople finally dispersed, Happy Harry went up the hillside.

"I thought that went well," Robert said.

"Hell, everybody in this city wants hope," Sturdley said. "Including me." He aimed an annoyed eye at his gigantic protege. "I noticed however, that the whole section I wrote about the distinctive costumes you'd wear disappeared from your speech."

"Sturdley, we don't want to wear your distinctive costumes. We don't need them." Robert clapped a hand to his 132-inch chest. "Maurice and I stand out in a crowd as we are."

"But when there are more of you—"

Robert's eyes glittered. "You've found John Cameron?"

"Not yet. But my people—"

"We can cross that river when we come to it."

Sturdley pulled out some papers from his jacket pocket. "At least look at the designs. You might find clothes useful—if only for the pockets."

Robert frowned. "Pockets?"

"Built-in pouches for carrying things."

The giant shrugged. "We have nothing to carry."

"What about your precious cards?"

Robert and Maurice glanced at their only possession: the pack of oversized cards. It lay in the middle of their boulder table, neatly held down by a rock about the size of Harry's head.

"Who would disturb them?" Maurice asked, "knowing they are ours?"

Sturdley had to admit defeat, at least for the present, but he felt better when he got the chance to tune in on the evening newscasts. The man on the street was solidly behind what the Heroes were trying to do. But *First News* had an unexpected reaction from the Policemen's Benevolent Association—the union for New York's cops. Leslie Ann Nasotradere conducted the interview, shamelessly egging on the union man to make inflammatory statements.

"The thin blue line has always been there to stand between the people and crime—little guys protecting the little guy." The union rep might have been a little more convincing without the heavy jowls. He looked like a big, fat guy who hadn't been "on the firing line," as he put it, for years.

"It's been our honor and privilege to serve the City of New York." Pinkness appeared on the rep's face, contrasting with the blue of his five-o'clock shadow. "And it's been our honor and privilege to carry guns. We don't think some oversized vigilantes should be telling us how to enforce the law—or trying to get us disarmed."

Leslie Ann, wearing less makeup than usual and with her hair pulled back in a tight bun, then took her viewers on a tour of police headquarters. Her cameraman dwelt on the huge piles of weapons confiscated by the forces of law and order.

The story ended and now they were covering the latest Balkan troubles. Harry Sturdley breathed a long sigh. He'd been warned that Nasotrudere could be a dangerous enemy. Now it looked as if she'd found herself some allies for an anti-hero campaign.

Antony Carron tapped the button on his remote, and the TV screen he and his associates had been watching went blank.

"It seems our informant was correct." Carron's dark eyes swept the group of men who stood beside him. They were a motley crew of career criminals, totally loyal to—and scared witless by—Antony Carron. He had an aquiline, almost Arabic nose, and a complexion like cafe au lait. He could be Sicilian or he could be Jamaican. His followers didn't know. All they knew was that they worked for the gun king of New York City.

"It was distressing enough that these giants intercepted the cargo being brought in by young Mr. Blood," Carron said. "But now it seems that we'll face a competition between the giants and police to accumulate the biggest collection of street guns."

"That sticks us in the middle," Joey Santangelo observed. "We'll get squeezed from both sides."

Carron's glance was so sharp that Santangelo

stepped back. Joey-boy was tough—he'd worked in lots of local crews and had made his bones with one of the old-fashioned dons' outfits, but the ruthlessness in his present master's eyes was enough to make him quail.

"Nobody squeezes us." Carron's voice was like a hammer slamming on steel. "We'll have to take care of these so-called heroes."

His eyes narrowed. "They've been very adept so far at using the media. But if they were to fail, very publicly . . ."

CHAPTER 12

Peg Faber was feeling grubby and exhausted. The flight to Washington had been crowded, the one to Charlotte bumpy. The rental car awaiting them had been cramped. It seemed to pant its way up the hills of West Virginia as Peg drove.

Was it Twain who said that if you really wanted to know someone go traveling with them? She'd learned two important things about her fellow searchers. Marty Burke was terrified of flying. He'd gotten sodden drunk on both planes and was now sleeping it off in the back seat. Elvio Vital had the worst map-reading skills in the world. Thanks to his navigation, they'd gotten off the interstate at the wrong exit and had wandered for hours on back roads.

Night had fallen by the time they finally passed a freshly painted sign announcing "KOKOMO, the tourist capital of Southern West Virginia."

Burke stirred bleary-eyed in the back. "Are we there?"

"Almost," Peg said, pulling up in front of a log cabin hostelry called the KoKoMo-tel.

Elvio stared at the flashing neon sign. "We're staying here?"

"It's the only place in town, unless you want to board with one of the local families." Peg was not in a mood to discuss things. What she wanted, in order of importance, was a cold drink, a hot meal, a warm bath, and a peaceful night's sleep.

They walked into the motel office to be greeted by a broad man with a balding head. "Welcome to Kokomo!" he said in an expansive voice. "I'm Hal Cameron, your host, and the mayor of this fine town."

"Not exactly a full-time job, eh?" Burke noted sardonically.

"We're a town on the move, though," the man behind the desk told them. "Changed our name this year. Used to be Cameron Corners. But we decided that sounded a bit too rural."

"Yeah," Burke agreed. "Kokomo's a lot more sophisticated."

"Glad you like it," Hal Cameron said. "I picked it out myself."

Peg, however, seized on the man's name. "Cameron? We're looking for a coworker—a friend—by that name."

Hal Cameron's eyes sharpened. "Looking for? This Cameron in some kind of trouble, Missy?"

Peg shook her head. "We need his help in a business deal, but he's left unexpectedly. We thought he might have come back here. His name is John."

"Lot of Camerons in this town, ma'am," their host said. "Lots of Johns, too. I can do some checking in my official capacity tomorrow. And, of course, we can check unofficially in the Mountain Rest, that's our local night spot, just down the hall."

The echo of loud country-western music suggested where the Mountain Rest might be found.

"Do you serve food there?" Peg asked.

"Damn good food," Hal Cameron told them. "My wife has a reputation round the county."

"Let's check it out after we get our keys," Peg said. "I think you have a reservation for us."

"Yes, ma'am," Hal Cameron said. "Called in this afternoon. You have cabins ten and eleven."

Peg took the keys and led the way to the Mountain Rest. The bar was crowded, and there were plenty of occupied tables, as well. They took a booth, Burke squeezing in beside Peg.

"Hill rats," he muttered through a mouthful of honey-fried chicken. "The people that time forgot. At least, the twentieth century forgot 'em." He washed the chicken down with a bottle of beer and ordered another one.

"Hey," Peg said. "I grew up in a small hill town, too. Western Pennsylvania. My folks didn't think the big city had so much to offer. They weren't happy when I left for New York. But that's where publishing is." She glanced owlishly at the bottle of beer in front of her. Was it the West Virginia water or her fatigue that was making her talk like this?

"So you started out in a hick town, huh?" Burke pressed, leaning over her. "Was it as small as this burg?"

"No. It was a college town. Dad taught English."

"Taming the barbarians," Burke guffawed. "You did the right thing, heading for civilization."

"Right now, civilization for me would be a comfortable bed," Peg said, stifling a yawn.

"Yeah," Burke said. "You have a pleasant night, Elvio."

Elvio Vital, who had almost been going into a doze over his plate, blinked awake. "¿Que? What did you say, Burke?"

Marty Burke was poking a possessive finger into Peg's ribs. "Maybe you thought I was out of it, but I didn't miss the action at the check-in, doll." He slid an arm around Peg's shoulders. "Two cabins. Ten and Eleven. One for Elvio, one for you and me, you little minx."

Peg was now wide awake. "When I decided to go off to civilization, as you put it, my folks were kind of nervous about me living along in a big city. So I did something to make them feel better."

Taking hold of the hand dangling down from her shoulder in search of lusher regions, she yanked Burke's arm straight out. Then she twisted to smash her other elbow into the fleshy part of Burke's forearm, slamming it against the back of the booth. "I learned karate."

"Jesus Christ!" Burke shrieked, cradling an arm that had suddenly gone dead. "What the hell did you do? I draw with this hand."

"Well, you won't be doing much with it tonight," Peg told him. "But then you'll have a roommate around to help you. You won't mind lending him a hand if he needs it, will you, Elvio?"

Vital ran a hand over his moustache to hide his smile. "Of course not, Peg."

"Good." Peg rose from the table. "Here's the key to

your room, and the key to the car." She hefted her shoulderbag. "Everything I need, I've got in here."

The artists watched in silence as Peg walked away. Elvio Vital hid his smile with less and less success. Finally Burke burst out, "Oh, and I bet you never thought of it, either."

"Maybe I did, my friend," Vital admitted. "But I have a higher regard for my extremities."

The next morning, Peg arrived in the restaurant to find the artists already eating breakfast. Whenever Burke bent his elbow to bring a forkful of eggs to his lips, he winced.

"Oh, stop being a baby," Peg admonished him. "When they demonstrated that move on *me*, I was back to throwing guys over my hip fifteen minutes later."

Hal Cameron came over. "Soon as you folks are finished with breakfast, we can go over to the municipal building."

Kokomo's municipal offices occupied the most solid building on Main Street, a former bank. The town records were kept in the old vault. Hal Cameron had already been shown his distant cousin's application form, so he knew the birth date to look for.

"No John Cameron listed for June 12, 1972," he said in bafflement. "Nor in the month before or after that date."

He riffled through the card files. "In fact, we don't even have any John Camerons listed as being born within five years of that time." His eyebrows rose. "Sure you got the right name and the right town?"

"It's here on the form." Peg unfolded the application. Under it was Elvio's sketch.

"That the fella there?" the mayor said, catching sight of the picture. Peg handed it over.

Hal Cameron carefully scrutinized the pencil sketch, frowning. Calling out to the town clerk, he said, "Effie, give the sheriff a call."

Kokomo's sheriff was hardly the usual yokel stereotype. He stood thin and ramrod-straight in knife-pressed khakis. Peg almost expected him to salute as he strode into the vault.

Hal Cameron held out the sketch. "Look familiar to you, Hobart?"

Sheriff Hobart's sandy eyebrows knit together. "Yes. A year and a half ago. That vagrant who was camping in the old Cameron place."

"The one in the holler?"

"No, the one down by the river."

The mayor gave Peg a lopsided smile. "Problem when you got so many Camerons around, you get lots of abandoned places where Camerons used to live."

A year and a half ago, Peg thought, glancing at the starting date on the application form. *That was about five months before our John Cameron appeared at the Fantasy Factory.*

"So you're saying you arrested this man as a vagrant?" Peg said.

The sheriff shook his head. "Gave us the slip. Don't know how. I had people front and back of that old farmhouse, but somehow he got away."

Just like he got out of the apartment with one guarded door, Peg thought.

She frowned. What had started out as grabbing a kid without a telephone had turned into a locked-door mystery. John Cameron had gone from an amiable boob to an escape artist with an ever-deepening air of mystery. For what must have been the hundredth time, Peg's mind went back to the painting in the day-care center; the two giants standing among the trees. He'd drawn the picture months before Robert and Maurice arrived. Had he seen them before? Where?

A niggling thought pierced her brain: she couldn't even prove he'd been on this planet more than a year and a half ago.

Peg shook her head, sending her red curls bobbing. *Get a grip,* she reproved herself. *This is John Cameron we're talking about, after all.*

"One more game, Maurice," Robert said, shuffling the cards. "Then we'll go off on patrol."

Brilliant spring sunshine fell on the promontory in New York's Central Park that the Heroes called home. Water droplets sparkled like diamonds on the green grass. There had been a sprinkle of rain the night before. Maurice had taken the cards inside his aura to keep them dry.

Robert squared off the cards and put them on the center of the boulder table. "I heard an interesting thing this morning," he said. "About you."

Maurice looked a little wary as he cut the cards.

"It seems you've made a new friend on your solo patrols." Robert dealt the cards with precision, his blue eyes drilling into the fine-boned features of his companion.

"I was only talking," Maurice said defensively.

"Talking with a rival of Sturdley's," Robert prodded. "Someone from this Dynasty Comics."

"He wanted to know if we had signed anything with

Sturdley's company." Maurice looked up, his voice growing defiant. "And we haven't."

"But we do have an agreement with Sturdley, depending on whether he can find this office boy who brought us here," Robert pointed out. "What do the Dynasty people offer?"

"Most of it I couldn't understand," Maurice admitted. "Something about better percentage on the back end, superior artists . . . it didn't make any sense." Still not touching his cards, Maurice leaned over the table. "But they promised us our own Hall, Robert! They would have it built to our size. We would have our own couches. They even promised us servants!"

"Empty words, Maurice." Robert made a dismissive gesture. "We need more than people to clean a house or tend its grounds. Our goal is to bring more of our kind to this world. To do that, we need the Lesser called John Cameron—and *Sturdley* is the one who can offer Cameron's services. Not his competition."

"Sturdley is not all-powerful in this world," Maurice sulked. "He's just a minor man of business."

"All the better for our purposes," Robert responded. "He can be controlled through his desire to make a profit."

They sat in silence for a while, the two hands of cards lying unregarded between them.

Finally, Robert asked, "Have you agreed to terms yet?"

"No—not yet," Maurice said in grudging tones.

Robert picked up his cards, reordering them in his hands. His attention seemed to be totally on his actions as he spoke.

"To do that, you would have to break our partnership. And if that happened, I would find it necessary to break your arms, your legs . . . possibly your neck."

Placing his cards face-down on the boulder, Robert leaned to one side, taking up a handful of the pebbles they used as chips.

"The offer from Dynasty would give us certain comforts for the present," Robert went on in the same quiet, deliberate tone. "But with Sturdley, we would have a future. Only his worker can open the way to home. Through Sturdley, we will have companions, females—a chance for progeny. The opportunity to settle a virgin world."

"*If* Sturdley can find this person and persuade him to meet the terms of the agreement," Maurice said sulkily.

"And if that happens, wouldn't it be far better than the inducements these others are offering?" Robert said. "I thought you were a better gambler than that, Maurice."

At last, Robert met his companion's eyes. "Remember this. For my plan, Sturdley and his servant are indispensable." Robert's eyes were like flat blue stones. "But you, my dear Maurice, are not."

He picked up his cards.

"Dealer takes two."

CHAPTER 13

"Well, I just hope you're happy now," Marty Burke fumed. The artist had been venting his venom on the rest of Sturdley's searchers all during the trip back to Charlotte and on the commuter plane to D.C. He was so annoyed, he hadn't even thought to get scared on the flight.

On the whole, Peg decided that she preferred him drunk and dozing in his seat.

The plane landed at National Airport, where they faced an hour's layover before the next New York shuttle. Burke made blasphemous comments under his breath, eager to get back to New York and his drawing board.

Peg's own feelings fell somewhere between frustration and pique. She found herself even more interested now than she'd been when they started. "What is it about John Cameron?" she muttered.

"He's a man of mystery," Elvio Vital said lightly.

"Yeah, well, you two can form his fan club. I've got work to do when we get back, and I don't intend to waste any more time on this loser."

For Burke, the best they'd gotten out of this trip was that Cameron almost had a criminal record. He didn't know how that could help Leslie Ann Nasotrudere, but he'd make sure she got the info.

The thought of criminal records set Burke's mind to work. "Wait a second," he said. "I have this contact, see? This guy loves my work. But he also loves mysteries—he can get all the dirt we need on Cameron." Marty Burke puffed up like a toad on steroids.

"And who is this master detective?" Elvio asked.

"My pal's a fed," Burke offered casually.

"FBI?" Peg asked, a bit impressed despite herself.

"Well, he works in their computer section," Burke admitted. "But that's what we need right now. He can call up the whole paper trail on Cameron."

As Burke headed for the pay phones, digging out change, Elvio said, "It's a shame you didn't think of this contact before. We might have saved a day's travel."

Peg made a face. "By the time we were in the air, he was already half sloshed."

Burke spoke into the phone. "Miles, Marty Burke. Yeah, that's right. Been a while since that convention. Remember how you told me that if I ever needed dirt on anyone, you were the one to call?"

Burke's face went sour. "You certainly did say that, you little weasel. Don't give me that 'I must have been drunk at the time' crap. You promised me I could depend on you."

An angry flush covered the artist's face. "You were talking pretty big, there in the Bongo Room. But now all I'm getting is whining about how you might lose your job. Look, this is important to me. I'm trying to find this guy, and if I don't do it soon, *Latter-Day Breed* is *never* going to come out."

That seemed to have some effect. Burke listened for a moment, then said, "That's right man, I need you. I need your help bad."

More listening. Peg watched as Burke's lips grew tighter and tighter. "All right then, what's it worth to you?"

Elvio leaned forward to whisper in her ear. "Obviously a very close, warm friendship."

"Soulmates," she whispered back.

At last, the haggling was done. Burke fed his connection the meager facts they had on John Cameron. "He's tall, about six foot two—well, that's tall to *me*. Whaddya mean, almost anything is tall to me? He's fat, about two-hundred and ten pounds—"

"I wouldn't say he was that fat," Peg said. "More like husky."

Burke paid no attention. "Baby face. Brown hair. Eyes?" He turned to the others.

"Dark," Peg said. "Brown?"

"Very dark blue," Elvio disagreed. "Or a deep purple."

"Really?" Peg said. "I never looked that closely."

"Do you people mind?" Burke yelled. "Dark eyes. According to his job application, he listed June 12, 1972 as his birthday. Me, I thought he looked younger. Also, he listed a town called Cameron Corners as his birthplace, but that turns out to be phony."

There was a moment's pause. Then, "Fingerprints!" Burke burst out. "Where the hell do you think we'd get his fingerprints? This is a comics company, not a nuclear research facility. All right, all right. His last known address was in Astoria, Queens." He rattled off the address from the application, and also the Social Security number that John had scrawled there.

"That's about all we've got. Can you turn your computers to work on it? Oh, thanks," he said sourly.

Burke looked over at the others. "He says the social security number better be good. Otherwise there should be only a hundred thousand people—give or take—who would match our physical description."

"That narrows it down," Elvio muttered.

"We do have the sketch of John," Peg pointed out.

"Think we can get the use of a fax machine around here?" Burke said dubiously, scanning the nearby airline booking desks.

After a little negotiation, Peg managed to get to an office fax and transmitted the picture to the FBI man. She also got permission to leave the office phone number for return calls. Then they sat down to wait. They had missed their scheduled flight by the time the phone rang.

Burke snatched the receiver up. "Hello! What? Yes. Yes, we'll accept." He put his hand over the speaker. "The weasel reversed the charges!" he muttered to the others. "Talk about covering your ass!"

Then he was speaking again. "Hello, Miles, watcha got for us? Uh-huh." He glanced over. "He's checked the civil, criminal, and tax records of all the John Camerons in America. He even accessed the FBI's fingerprint computer." Burke went back to talking into the phone. "Great work, Miles. But what's the bottom line? What have you got on our guy?"

He listened for another moment, then went bright red. "*What*? What do you mean? Then how do I know you did anything? You could just be yanking my chain!

I hope you don't expect to see anything from me for this kind of work. . . . Yeah? Same to you, asshole!"

Marty Burke slammed the phone down. "He's got zip. According to him, there's no John Cameron in the Washington computers who fits our profile."

"Well, it was a pretty sketchy profile," Elvio had to admit.

"What about taxes?" Peg asked. "We pay withholding on him . . ."

"Yeah," Burke said in annoyance. "But it turns out the Social Security number he used belongs to a dead guy."

"The Man Who Never Was," Peg Faber muttered.

The two artists both stared at her.

"What?" Burke said.

"It's a book I read when I was a kid," Peg explained, "about a trick back in World War II. The Allies sent a dead body with false papers to fool the Germans into shifting their defense. They created an entire fake identity for the dead man." Her heart-shaped face puckered in a frown. "Just like John Cameron has apparently done for himself."

"Except he's alive," Burke said. "You know, that's a pretty neat idea. I could use that in *Latter-Day Breed.* Thanks, doll." He went to put his arm around her, abruptly winced, and put his hand down.

Peg's shoulders slumped in defeat as she walked over to the telephone. "I might as well let Mr. Sturdley know we've hit the final dead end."

Harry Sturdley found himself busily juggling a collection of phone calls. It seemed that every time he got onto one line, Eddie Walcott was buzzing him with some new disaster.

His first call was from a disaffected artist at Dynasty Comics, passing along office scuttlebutt on Dynasty's giant negotiations.

"The dark haired one—Maurice—isn't talking to our rep anymore," the artist said. "In fact, the last time the rep saw him, Maurice began—"

The intercom buzzer blared. "Call for you on line three," Eddie Walcott announced. "Saul Marranais from Marranais Mode Clothing."

"Ralph, can you hold on for a minute?" Sturdley put his spy on hold, and picked up the other call. "Saul, how are we doing? Almost ready?"

"Mr. Sturdley, I had to be desperate to do this." Marranais' voice was almost a moan.

"My cousin said you *were* desperate—you've got nothing going on at that factory of yours, and you're stuck with a huge overstock of Spandex just as the bottom has fallen out of the bicycle pants market."

"You don't have to rub it in," Marranais said. "It's just that your designs—"

"What's wrong with our designs?" Sturdley barked. "I'll have you know that my people have come up with some of the most successful costumes—"

"But they weren't meant to be made!" Marranais burst out. "They're fine as drawings, but as a practical guide for the cutting and fitting, they're useless!"

"That's where your expertise comes in," Sturdley said.

"We don't have any expertise in making twenty-foot-long clothes!" Marranais responded furiously. "Maybe you should have contacted the company that makes the balloons for the Thanksgiving Day Parade!"

"As far as I know, they still have work," Sturdley replied. "Or at least they will as long as Macy's doesn't go bankrupt. Look at it this way, Saul," he wheedled, "when this is done, you're going to have a twenty-foot advertisement you can point to."

"I can see it now," the clothing maker moaned. "They'll call it Marranais' Folly."

"Mr. S." Eddie Walcott's voice sounded over the intercom.

"Hold for a second, Saul," Sturdley said. "What is it, Eddie?"

"Another call from Cousin Louie."

"Perfect," Sturdley muttered. "Do you have a clue as to which one?"

"Not really," Eddie admitted. "He keeps mentioning something about Latex—"

"Tell him I'll call back. And Eddie—no more calls."

Happy Harry punched one of the glowing buttons on his phone. "Saul?"

"No, this is Ralph."

"Right. What did Maurice do to this guy?"

"He chased him almost to Fifth Avenue. Told him to get lost and never bother him again."

Sturdley smiled. This, at least, was good news.

"I hope you remember this, Sturdley. I want a good berth over there when my contract is up with these clowns."

"The best, Ralph. We're starting up a new series with the Glamazon, and—"

Sturdley heard the receiver on the other end being knocked against a desk. "Something wrong with this phone, Harry?" Ralph asked, getting back on the line. "I asked for a *good* job."

"Wiseguy," Sturdley groused.

"I'll tell you more if I hear anything," Ralph said. "Gotta go. Dirk Colby's making his monthly round of the peons."

The artist hung up, and Sturdley clicked onto the other call. "Sorry about that, Saul. I'm sure you can handle the technical challenges. It will be a triumph. By the way, did I mention that the costume needs pockets?"

There was dead silence from the other end of the line.

"Pockets?" Saul Marranais said, hysteria edging his voice. "Did you say pockets? This is a skintight suit! Where are we supposed to put pockets?"

"Well, one pocket, then," Sturdley said. "It should be big enough to fit something . . ." He estimated the size of a playing card, then tripled it. "Oh, about seven and a half inches by ten and a half inches."

More silence from Saul Marranais.

Outside, his office, Sturdley heard the phone ring and Eddie's voice respond. "Oh, hi, Peg. Gee, I dunno. Mr. Sturdley's on the other line—"

"You can do it, Saul," Harry said quickly, then hung up.

"Eddie!" he called. "Is that Peg Faber? Put her on!"

Peg was not her usually perky self. "Mr. Sturdley, I'm calling from the airport in Washington. My hunch didn't turn out, I'm afraid. John's not in West Virginia. In fact, we're not even sure if his name is really John." She gave a condensed report of the team's search.

Sturdley sank back in his chair. Well, that was it.

John Cameron apparently didn't want to be found. That meant his original deal with the giants was down the tubes.

"I know you tried, Peg. Head back home."

"There's one more thing I can do," his assistant said, gulping. "I can make one last check of the hospitals—and morgues."

Sturdley frowned. "You sure you want to do that? Maybe I should send the guys on that."

"I want to do it, Harry. I've *got* to know what happened to John."

"Okay, then," Sturdley said with a sigh. "I'll expect you sometime in the afternoon."

He hung up, then picked up the phone again, dialing the number of Marranais Mode Fashions. The costume was the only card he had left. He'd have to sweet-talk Marranais into getting it ready as soon as possible.

The next day was a trial for Happy Harry Sturdley. His media watch was a bust. Heavy news days had pushed the heroes off the tube. The big interest now was a series of bloody gun battles going on in the northern tip of Manhattan. The pictures were like something out of a war zone—dozens hit with sprays of automatic weapons fire.

"Maybe we should get our boys to patrol up that way," Sturdley said to himself.

That was, of course, if Maurice and Robert were still the Fantasy Factory's boys.

He arrived early at the office to find Marty Burke on the point of murdering Fabian Thibault. "You think you could slip this crap in behind my back?" Burke yelled, rattling a pile of illustration boards. He looked ready to burst out of his black suit.

"Hey, they need a story ASAP, and I had this one already penciled." Thibault's sandy moustache was bristling, but he was retreating from the furious Burke.

"Yeah, I remember—I turned it down a year ago, and it doesn't look any better today. It doesn't follow anything that's going on in the story arc—"

"Wait, I fixed that. I've got a reference to whatsername, Echo, dying. It's on the fourth page."

Burke turned to the appropriate page and scanned it. The veins began standing out on the side of his head. "This is it? 'Echo was great undercover, but now she's underground.'"

"Well, you know, they were lovers, under the covers, and she was a spy—"

Burke crumpled up the boards. From the look on his face, he was obviously wishing he had Thibault's neck in his hands.

"Hey, you're ruining my work!"

"Ruining your work?" Burke's voice rose. "Ruining your *work*? What do you think you're doing to the effort I've put into this title over the last year? It's taken the better part of nine months to kill off the cheap jokes Mr. Pain used to mouth. I'm away for a couple of days, and you've got him saying something stupid about the woman he loves— right after her death!"

Burke stopped crumpling and began tearing up the illustrations.

"Hey!" Thibault took a couple of steps forward but stopped before he got in range of Burke's fists. They were about the same height, but Marty had a good thirty pounds on the slender Thibault.

Torn illustration board filled the air like confetti as Burke threw the shredded artwork at his replacement artist.

Thibault noticed Sturdley taking in the spectacle and turned to him. "The guy is crazy, Harry. He just destroyed the fill-in story I did."

"It was crap!" Burke yelled.

"I'm putting in for payment on it," Thibault said. "And don't expect me to do anything more to help out the Genius there. He can draw himself out of this corner. He knows how to dog it—we'll probably wind up with a book sporting one panel per page."

"And it would still sell better than anything you've done in the last fifteen years, you has-been," Burke shouted. He too turned to Harry. "I'm taking *Mr. Pain* back. I don't care if I have to pull a week of all-nighters; I'm not going to let Thibault screw up the book."

"And what about *Glamazon?*" Harry asked.

Burke hesitated for a second, then his jaw jutted out. "I'll do that, too. But you'll have to get off my back about *Latter-Day Breed*. I won't be in—I'll work at my studio, instead."

Sturdley assented with a shrug. That meant a good week without Burke around. In his eyes, that was a major plus.

The rest of the morning passed in a blur of meetings and phone calls, mainly to Saul Marranais. The costume would be ready as promised.

When the lunch run went off to Central Park, Sturdley sent a message asking the giants to come down to talk with him. He skipped lunch himself and sat down to wait.

"Where is it?" Sturdley asked for at least the thousandth time. He reached out to tap the intercom button, then pulled his hand back. Poor Eddie Walcott must have gotten the question about five hundred times already. He could only try to be patient. It was supposed to arrive before the giants did.

The intercom buzzed. "Mr. S.," Eddie reported, "it's here."

A crew from the mail room came staggering in under a huge, ungainly box, cobbled together from a few large cartons.

"Get it open!" Sturdley said.

Box cutters flicked open in several of the mail guys' hands. "Careful!" Sturdley yelled. "I don't want you ruining what's inside."

They finally got the top off, and white Spandex overflowed into the room.

"What the—" Eddie Walcott said.

Sturdley smiled with all the pride of an expectant father. "It's a costume," he said. "Make sure it's all here."

They began spreading out the Spandex, filling the room. Here were the leggings, there was the top. Sturdley noticed that Marranais had even managed to add a patch breast pocket.

The mailroom staffer half inside the box called out, "Now it's all blue cloth."

"Be very careful with it," Sturdley said. "That's the cape."

They wrestled out a billowing mass of Spandex that looked more like half a parachute. There was no surface in Sturdley's office that wasn't covered in fabric.

"Good work, men," Happy Harry said. "Now get out of here."

He went to open the window to prepare for the giants' arrival.

Suddenly, a horrible, vertiginous sensation gripped him. He staggered, clutching at the windowframe as the floor below him seemed to disappear into a bottomless gulf.

Slowly, the void passed away. Harry opened his eyes to find his hands in a white-knuckled grip on the casement. He forced his fingers to unclamp.

That'll teach me for passing on lunch, he thought. *This is not the time to get giddy. I've got too much riding on the next few minutes.*

Downstairs, Peg Faber exited a cab, shouldered her bag, and marched into the building lobby.

She felt as if she were going to face a firing squad as she strode past the emerging lunchtime crowd. All she had to show for a frustrating morning of checking with police and medical types was more wasted time. Zero. Zip. The big goose egg. She'd have to face Mr. Sturdley and tell him she'd screwed up again.

Peg stood aside as a flood of people poured from one of the elevators. One of the Fantasy Factor gofers on his way out stopped to hold the doors open while she stepped into the empty car. She barely acknowledged him.

The guy let go, and the elevator doors began to shut. They were almost together when a hand appeared in the tiny space remaining, tapping the rubber safety bumpers.

The doors shot open. "What kind of stupid—" Peg began sharply. Then her voice deserted her.

Standing in the opening was a familiar rumpled figure, with a familiar baby face.

John Cameron.

And he *did* have purple eyes.

CHAPTER 14

"Where have you been?" Peg Faber shrieked, hurling herself at John Cameron. She didn't know whether to hit him or hug him. At the last minute, she decided on the hug.

The shock of being struck by one hundred and three pounds of warm, well-curved femininity turned John Cameron's face pink and sent him staggering back a couple of steps into the middle of the lobby.

Behind Peg, the elevator doors closed, while its neighbor arrived at ground level. Among those disembarking were Elvio Vital in search of lunch, and Marty Burke, toting a thick block of official Fantasy Factory illustration board.

Burke got about four steps from the elevator when he recognized the guy Peg Faber seemed to be climbing onto. "Hey!" he began, turning toward them.

Elvio Vital hooked Burke's arm, pulling him away. A smile curved his moustache, part indulgent, part bittersweet. He recognized the look in Peg Faber's eyes. She probably didn't even know it yet. But he did.

"Let them be," Elvio told the other artist. "She'll bring him up in a moment." He smiled. "Besides, I thought you didn't want to waste any more time on him. You've got a date with the Glamazon, don't you?"

They walked away, leaving Peg Faber to do her best at throwing her arms around John Cameron—an armful of surprisingly solid muscle.

"Where have you been?" she demanded again. "I've been worried sick about you."

"Ah—ah," John babbled as if he'd suddenly misplaced his voice or his brain. "Y—you were?"

Peg pulled herself away a little shakily, putting her hands on her hips. "I thought you'd gotten yourself killed! We were checking the hospitals and the morgues, we had the police out, even the FBI, and I went down to West Virginia . . ."

The spate of words ended. Peg drew herself up and vigorously shook her head, as if by tousling her curls she could restore some kind of order to her mind.

She reached out and touched the elevator button. "Mr. Sturdley's been going crazy trying to get hold of you. He's had me out looking, and Elvio, and Marty Burke."

"Oh," John replied.

Peg waited until they were in the relative privacy of the elevator before she started talking again. "Mr. Sturdley's in the middle of the biggest deal he's ever made, talking with those giants you brought here. You did do that, didn't you?"

No answer.

"Well, that's what the giant called Robert told Harry. He needed you, and you just—just disappeared yourself."

For the third time she asked, "Where were you?"

"I had to get away for a while," John finally said.

"Away where?"

"Just—away."

Peg began to think her first instinct had been right. She should have hit him.

They finished their elevator ride in a mood of silent constraint. But as the doors opened, Peg abruptly hooked her arm through his and began marching him down the hallway to the executive offices. John seemed to be walking in a daze, his color still high.

You'd think he'd never been this close to a girl in his life, Peg thought. She glanced over at the goofy expression on his face. That couldn't be right, could it?

Peg rounded the corner to find Eddie Walcott at her desk and the door to Harry Sturdley's office closed. Eddie shot to his feet as Peg steered John to the doorway.

"He's in a meeting!" her replacement bleated.

"Whoever he's seeing, he'll want to see us more," Peg said. She threw the door open and proceeded to trip over a tremendous swath of white cloth. It was a lucky thing she was holding onto John, or she'd have landed flat on her face.

Peg stared around the office. There was cloth everywhere. It reminded her of her grandmother's house when Gran used to go away for the summer. Out of the attic came dust covers for every item of furniture in the place.

But this fabric wasn't for keeping off dust. It was Spandex, in what appeared to be mounds and streamers leading to the window.

Harry Sturdley was almost out on the window ledge, flapping some of the fabric in the air.

"Feel it, just feel it," he shouted in a wheedling voice. "Imagine the sensation of this next to your skin."

"Sturdley," an annoyed rumble came from outside. "No!"

"It's great material," Sturdley persisted. "One size fits all."

"We have no interest in this costume," the rumble returned. "We know the boy is in this building."

Peg clutched John's arm tighter. The giant was right outside!

Still fixated on his sales pitch, Sturdley pulled on a huge swath of blue Spandex. "At least take a look at the cape. Do you know what this cost me? Besides, capes always make people look taller."

"We know the boy is here," Robert repeated.

"Harry!" Peg called in a stage whisper.

Sturdley turned around, his gray hair a little disheveled. For a second, he froze, partly in embarrassment, partly in indignation at finding uninvited guests barging into his office.

Then it finally penetrated. Sturdley's eyes went wide. He yelled, "Excuse me a minute!" out the window, then stumbled across the Spandex to get to the door.

Sturdley grabbed John's free hand, began pumping it, and propelled the three of them out of his office.

"Kid," he said as soon as he had the door closed behind them, "am I glad to see you! Where have you been?"

"Away," Peg said, a bit of tartness in her voice.

John Cameron was looking over Sturdley's shoulder at the closed door. No, he seemed to be looking through it, maybe through the outer wall of the building, as well, and toward the giants beyond.

"Kid! John!" Sturdley said. "Talk to me. Don't get that spaced-out look now. I've been tap dancing with that pair of big lugs outside for too long, trying to keep this deal alive."

He leaned closer, his eyes burning into John's. "Now tell me the truth. The giants say they wouldn't be here without you. *Did* you bring them here?"

John Cameron looked very young as he nodded, almost like a kid admitting to raiding the cookie jar. "I didn't exactly mean to do it. It sort of happened after I opened the Rift."

"The Rift?" Happy Harry echoed.

"That's what I call it," John explained. "I don't really know what it is. But somehow I can use it, through some trick of my mind. The first couple of times I called it up, I got really scared. It was like this bottomless hole opening under my feet, and I'd feel real dizzy and sick . . ."

"Giddy," Sturdley said almost under his breath. "Like you were going to fall forever." He stared at John with an intensity that Peg found frightening.

John nodded, a little surprised at how Harry grasped what he was talking about. "That's exactly how I felt when I let myself go in. I dropped for what felt like eons, and then I found myself in another world."

He glanced at Peg. "That's why you couldn't find me, no matter how hard you tried. I went away through the Rift, to visit—someplace else."

"That's why the door was locked and the window untouched," Peg said numbly. "You dropped out through a hole in your mind."

John gave her an embarrassed grin. "I guess that's about the way of it."

"So it is you." Sturdley sounded fascinated, then his voice got sharper. "Unless you know somebody else who can do this trick."

John Cameron shook his head.

"Could you teach someone how to do it?"

"I don't think so." The boyish face looked confused.

"So, as far as you know, you're the only source," Sturdley seemed to be musing aloud.

"Of what?" John asked.

"Of giants." Happy Harry's voice got a little sharp. "That's my deal with Robert. He wants fifty of his people in this world—males and females. If we can do that, we can make comics about them—unlimited rights."

John's curiously unfinished features were twisted with a painful intensity as he looked into Harry's eyes. "Gosh, Mr. Sturdley," he finally blurted out. "Are you sure that's a good idea?"

Peg and Sturdley both looked at each other. Did anybody say "gosh" anymore?

"Good? It's a great idea. Think of it, kid. *Real, live superheroes*. It's the chance of a lifetime for comics, for the Fantasy Factory." His voice dropped away. "If we let those guys out there get away, they go to Dirk Colby, and we close up this place in about three months."

He wasn't going to let it go at that. "This city, this *world*, needs superheroes. Robert and Maurice have done a lot of good. They could do a lot more. And they can save this company. It's your choice, kid."

Sturdley reached up, putting a hand on John's shoulder. "You've got me over a barrel here. Tell you what I'll do. The first comic with the giants in it is bound to become the best-seller of all time. Peg tells me you can draw. I'll make you the artist on the book."

John shook his head. "Look, it's not that, Mr. Sturdley—"

"Then *what?*" Sturdley yelled, going from avuncular to homicidal. "I'm offering to make you a star. This should be your dream come true."

John Cameron looked down at his shoes. "Actually," he mumbled, "it's *your* dream come true."

Sturdley froze, hit with a pitch from left field. "What?" he finally said.

"Remember that staff meeting?" John said. "The one with the big fight? When I brought the coffee in, you wished there were real superheroes. So I tried to make that happen."

"You were going to make it happen for me by opening the Rift," Harry said, a little dazed.

"I knew about this world where there were giants with powers beyond"—John shrugged—"humans. So I tried to reach out to find someone who wanted to help people—"

"And you found Robert and Maurice," Sturdley finished.

John shook his head. "No. They pushed in from the other side. You see, they wanted to get away from their world. When I opened the Rift, they just—came through."

"And they've done wonderful things," Sturdley said. "They rescued a girl from a gang of crazy kids. They've stopped illegal guns from coming into the city. They've saved lives."

John looked questioningly at Peg.

"They've done all that, and more," she said with a nod.

"Kid—John," Sturdley said. "You say you brought these guys over because that was my wish. Well, this deal is the biggest wish of my life. Make it come real for me."

"You're sure?"

Sturdley became a father figure, patting John on the shoulder. "Trust me, son, I'm sure."

"Then I'll do whatever you want me to." John's head came up, the faraway look in his eyes. Faint fear showed on his face. "Anyway, I can't get away now. They know I'm here."

"And they'll be happy to know we've got a deal." Happy Harry turned to Peg. "Get up to McManus in Legal, and tell him we need the contracts he's been working on right now."

He patted John on the back. "You'll never regret this, kid."

Twenty minutes later, Robert stood frowning out on Park Avenue as he shuffled through sheaves of over-sized paper. "I don't like this fine print."

"It's twelve-point type." Sturdley threw up his hands. "And we did put it on eleven-by-seventeen paper."

Squinting, Robert continued to read suspiciously. "What's this clause here? 'All heroes will agree to comport themselves within the confines of the Comics Code with regard to violence, morality, and habiliment.'"

He looked at Peg. "What is 'habiliment'?"

Her eyebrows went up. "It's a term for attire, clothes."

Happy Harry shot her a dirty look.

Robert went berserk. "You're still trying to force us into those stupid costumes!"

"We need the costumes to make this work!" Harry shot back. "Comics characters have always worn costumes to make them stand out, to make them special. Even the giant characters."

Robert and Maurice glanced at each other. The blond giant's face was set. "I will not—"

"If you won't wear the costumes, your people aren't coming over." John Cameron's voice rose clear and firm. "Don't just read my lips, giant. Read my mind."

The bulky kid and the handsome giant stared into each others' eyes for a long moment.

"It wouldn't kill you to try it on," Sturdley said, breaking the tension.

Robert sighed, sending a breeze through the window. "Maurice! Try the foolish thing on."

Maurice broke into a pout. "Why me?" he whined.

"Because I asked you to."

Mumbling and swearing to himself, Maurice complied.

All traffic had ceased on Park Avenue with the appearance of the giants. Now the sidewalks jammed to overflowing as New Yorkers turned out in the thousands for the spectacle of a twenty-foot man getting dressed for the first time in his life.

"I think you should take your boots off before you pull on the pants. Also, it looks like you're putting them on backwards," Sturdley advised at Maurice's first attempt.

Luckily, the news cameras arrived after the more awkward stages were over. Maurice pulled the shirt on, patch pocket to the front. Then he attached the cape.

"Put you hands on your hips and take a deep breath," Sturdley directed.

Maurice did as he was asked.

A cheer rose from below as the news cameras taped it all.

"How does it feel?" Robert asked.

Maurice shrugged a couple of times, hitched his arms, and bowed his legs. "Constricting," was his single-word review.

"We'll get our tailors on it right away," Sturdley promised. "You look great—like a Hero."

He turned to his desk, now clear of fabric, opened the drawer, and took out an enormous pen. "It's supposed to be a novelty, but it really writes—and it's permanent ink."

Leaning against the side of the building, Robert signed the contract.

Harry Sturdley breathed a long sigh of relief. The Heroes were now officially a part of the Fantasy Factory.

CHAPTER 15

Robert passed the contracts through the windowframe. "All right, Sturdley, you've gotten what you wanted. When do we get what we need?"

Sturdley glanced at John Cameron, who only shrugged in reply. "Now, if you want it."

Robert's piercing blue eyes glittered. "Then I want it now."

John took a deep breath. His eyes seemed to go out of focus, as if he were contemplating the infinite. Harry Sturdley began to feel the first twinges of vertigo.

"Hold it a second!" he said. "Is it really such a good idea to do this in public?"

Robert frowned, struck by the thought. "You have a point, Sturdley." He glanced down at the crowd and the camera crews. "How will we do this?"

"Talk to them, get rid of the newspeople," Sturdley advised. "The cameramen will want to get the film back to their editors for the evening news, anyway. Next, head back up to Central Park and let this traffic unclog. John and I will meet you up there in two hours."

Robert frowned. "Why will you be there?"

"I thought I'd come along for the ride. You've seen my world; I'd like to see yours."

Robert's frown deepened. "That is—" He paused. "That is not wise. My world is considerably more . . . untamed than this one. If there were an accident"—he raised his eyebrows—"who on Earth would we deal with?"

Sturdley tried to be gracious about being denied his adventure. "Okay, I know when I'm beat," he grumped. "But I'd still like to see what happens. I'm going to feel it, anyway." Turning to John, he explained about his recent strange bouts of vertigo. "They must be tied to whenever you open this Rift of yours," he finished. "That's what Robert thinks."

"You can come into the Rift, if you want," John offered. "I've been thinking of ways to make the sensation a little less, uh, nauseating."

Robert turned to the crowd, and Sturdley had to take his turn talking to the representatives of the press. Behind the scenes, Peg and the rest of the staff were making frantic preparations for the advent of forty-eight gigantic new arrivals. They'd need food and a place to stay. The knoll in Central Park would get awfully crowded. And, of course, Harry put in an order for more uniforms. Saul Marranais didn't know whether to cheer or cry.

Frank McManus was able to suggest a temporary headquarters for the anticipated newcomers. "My aunt has a summer place in upper Westchester," he said.

"It's an old estate—walled—overlooking the Hudson. And it's only about an hour's drive from here."

Sturdley and John Cameron cabbed up to Central Park. "I'm going to suggest that Maurice patrol alone while we're away," Sturdley said. They already had come to the realization that they would be in the Rift for hours while Robert visited his homeworld. He'd have to find people and talk them into this venture.

"With luck, Maurice will draw attention away from us," Happy Harry added. "And it will be a chance to show off the new suit."

They arrived to find Robert eagerly awaiting them. Maurice, in the meantime, had gotten much more used to his costume. The giants agreed to follow Sturdley's plan.

The three waited while Maurice marched off across the park, heading north. Sturdley had mentioned the trouble in the northern neck of town, and Maurice promised to look into it.

When Maurice was out of sight, Robert led the way up the hill and into the covert of thick trees. "This should do well," he said. "No one can see us this far in."

John looked around and nodded. He took a deep breath, and his eyes went unfocused. Harry Sturdley felt a tickle deep within himself.

"I think it's better," John whispered, "if you closed your eyes."

Antony Carron dry-fired the Ingram MAC-10, then slammed the magazine home. It was a double magazine, two boxes of bullets taped back-to-back. Three seconds of fire could empty both magazines. Carron's people had four such guns. He hefted the MAC-10 in one hand. Ten pounds of pure murder.

He arranged his people behind the two front windows of the uptown tenement. Once upon a time, they'd let light into somebody's front parlor. Tonight, if his plans went right, they would let out 240 shards of sudden death.

Carron checked the sightlines, calculated arcs of fire, and gave his people detailed instructions. "Okay. The curtain goes up on our little drama at eight o'clock. Give it an hour to gather enough of a crowd. If we haven't lured a giant here by then, only Joey fires. One magazine, right, Joey?"

Joey Santangelo nodded.

"Then everyone gets upstairs to the second-floor rear apartment. There's a board laid from the back window to the building across the way. However it goes down, three seconds to fire, three upstairs, three across the bridge. You'll be out of here ten seconds after the first bullet flies. Understood?"

Carron looked over his troops, who signified their understanding—four grim, silent men, as nasty a group as could be assembled in this city.

"Pedro is upstairs with the girl. He'll start the ball rolling. You know your parts now, so I'll be leaving."

One of the hired hands, a big Dominican, went to follow him. Carron put up a hand. "No. All of you stay till this goes down."

"I need a beer," the big guy said.

"There's a well-stocked refrigerator in the kitchen," Carron told him. "But there's no phone, and no one goes out. I want no leaks."

"And who's going to make us follow the rules?"

"Joey?" Carron turned to his right-hand man. Santangelo produced a silent pistol.

"Shoot whoever wants to leave in the leg. If they still make trouble"—Carron shrugged—"go for the head."

Following John Cameron's advice, Harry Sturdley closed his eyes. A moment later, he was shaken by a milder version of the now-familiar nauseating vertigo, the sensation of falling. Then it went away.

He opened his eyes to find a marble floor under his feet. "Where?" he said, looking around.

The vista was strangely familiar yet alien. He'd been here hundreds of times in his life, yet never seen it like this.

They stood at the entrance to the main hall of Grand Central Station. But it was a Grand Central Station newly minted, as it must have looked when the place was built ninety years ago. The sandstone was clean, the marble shiny, the paint gleaming. The accretions—the shops, the grime—were gone.

So were the people. This was the titanic train station as newfound land, without a human footprint.

"My God," Sturdley breathed. His whisper reverberated off the vaulted ceiling high above them, crashing through the silence.

Even Robert was silent, dwarfed by the scale of the place.

They walked into the rotunda, their footsteps echoing and re-echoing in the vast space.

"This isn't real." Sturdley whispered, as if he feared to shatter the illusion.

"We're in the Rift," John explained. "I found I could

create a little bubble of reality in the void. Makes it easier to take."

Harry kept looking around. "Why did you choose this?"

John shrugged. "It's a good image for our minds to hold onto—you help to stabilize it, too." He grinned a little whimsically. "And it's the right kind of place—the Rift has a lot of destinations."

"You mean, like the crisis on alternate Earths?" Sturdley tried to get his mind around the idea. Did that mean there were infinite worlds of superheroes?

"Not exactly," John said. "I don't think they're alternate worlds, but they don't seem to be in other solar systems." He shrugged as he led them into the building's main rotunda. "I'm not sure *what* they are."

As they crossed the mammoth hall, Sturdley's eyes narrowed. There was something wrong with the scale at the far end. One of the passage mouths that should have led down to the train platforms was much larger than the others.

"That's the way to Robert's world," John said, seeming to sense an unspoken question.

He turned to look up at the giant. "We can't stay here in the Rift forever, you know. I'd say a time limit of four hours is enough for this visit."

"Will that be enough time?" Harry asked. "Or will we have to make several trips before you get all your people?"

"We'll see," Robert said quietly. "Depending on how conditions are, four hours may be all I'll need."

"Do you want me to return to the spot you left?" John asked.

Robert nodded. "That should be satisfactory."

"Whenever you're ready."

Robert started walking through the tunnel mouth, down the ramp. John stood very still. "Harry—your eyes."

Sturdley closed his eyes again, feeling a sudden chill as if the place where he stood had suddenly turned to vapor. For a second or two, he had that endless falling sensation.

Then John sighed, and Happy Harry felt firm marble beneath his feet again.

The kid looked down at Harry, a quizzical expression on his boyish features. "We could go now," he said. "Just leave him there. Left on his own, he could never come back."

"Are you nuts?" Harry's shriek seemed to clatter around the huge room. "We've got a deal! And in four hours, we'll have fifty of the greatest Herocs of all time—under contract! Dynasty will have to go into the toilet paper business!"

"Just a suggestion," John said.

Maurice had a long walk to the trouble spot Sturdley had described to him. The first part of the trek was across the parkland. But then the park ended, and Maurice was walking the city streets.

The buildings in this part of northern Manhattan were shorter than those farther south, and more worn. He saw traces of poverty and violence, and he felt the fear of the Lessers much more strongly.

He still had to walk a mile by his scale to reach his destination. That was no problem. Maurice moved with the gait of a practiced walker. But the costume he wore presented its own difficulties. It was still a constant surprise to feel the fabric rubbing against his skin. Certain spots chafed. He tried to adjust his aura to dissipate more heat. Even so, sweat began to gather and dampen areas.

And then there was the cape. Not only did its weight feel alien on his shoulders, but it kept brushing things, catching on them—the stoops of buildings, the branches of trees. Every gust of wind seemed to catch in its folds, tugging him a little off-balance. He tried to extend his aura to encompass the billowing cloth, but even with his enhanced powers, Maurice found this a strain. It slowed him down and started a pounding headache. In the end, he chose to put up with the aggravation rather than weaken himself.

Twilight had fallen by the time he reached the zone of action. To Maurice, the entire area was aboil with conflicting currents of anger, fear, violence, and an awful sense of morbid curiosity. All he had to do was proceed toward the highest-pitched swirl of emotion.

The storm of feelings centered on an old tenement building, five stories high. Once its facade had been of yellowish brick. Now glaring floodlights revealed every chip and grime stain.

Police cars blocked the ends of the street in front of the building, and blue-coated officers of the law swarmed on the sidewalk. As was common now, some shouted and made obscene gestures when they saw him. From others, however, he detected a certain relief at his appearance.

Far outnumbering the police were the countless bystanders, a crowd surging across the sidewalks and even into the street around the tenement building. Eddies in the current of humanity swirled around the vans where TV news crews aimed their cameras from vehicle roofs.

A somewhat harassed-looking officer, apparently in charge of the police, paused in his orders to stare up at Maurice.

"Nice tights," he said. "You look like something right out of a comic book."

From the undercurrent of thought, Maurice knew this was not a compliment.

"What's the problem, Captain?" he asked, plucking the officer's rank from his mind.

"We got a report of shots fired—sort of an everyday occurrence in this neighborhood. Apparently the shooter is in the front third-floor apartment. But he says he's got a hostage with him. I hear you guys can read minds, see through walls—want to have a go at it?"

Nodding, Maurice lowered his shields. Teeming thoughts chittered at the edges of his consciousness in a variety of languages. His immaterial senses warned of weapons all over the place, not merely in police hands. It would be easy enough to seize and destroy several guns, even caches of them, but he sensed the trouble that would cause. It would be like thrusting one's hand into a beehive. Wholesale stinging would begin. He glanced around the streets, too full of people. Weren't these bystanders aware of the violence that could be so quickly unleashed?

Then terror flared out of the worn building. "Yes," Maurice told the officer, "there's a hostage."

As if in response to his announcement, a window-shade suddenly flew up in the third-floor apartment. A man and a woman stood backlit. The man had one arm around the woman's neck, a pistol to her head.

"Yo, cops!" the man yelled into the street. "Get outta here!"

The dread from the woman held hostage seemed to stain the air.

Maurice took a step forward, then hesitated. He was too far away to reach for the woman's captor or extend any protection.

The building was the second in from the corner, and it quickly became evident that the hostage-taker had seen Maurice. "So you got one of those freaks with you, huh? Well, back off, giant. You come any closer and the woman gets it."

In the glare of the television lights, the gunman laughed at the discomfited titan. "Yeah, big man," he taunted. "Whatchoo gonna do now, huh? You may be bulletproof, but this girl ain't. And the people down there."

Below, the crowd reacted as if it were watching some sort of show. Behind the thin blue line holding them back, innumerable necks craned for a better view.

Maurice was pale with fury. No Lesser had ever dared talk to him this way. Still worse was the realization that all this was being captured by the cameras. But he knew that a frontal assault would only cost the girl her life, and threaten the assembled bystanders below with stray bullets. There seemed only one possible course.

The gunman continued to heckle Maurice as the giant turned back. "Yeah, back off, ya overgrown baby! You may be big, but you got the heart of a chicken!"

Maurice waited until he was out of sight of the gun-man, then turned a corner and dashed down the block. He circled to the street behind the tenement where the hostage scene was taking place. His only hope was that these older, squatter buildings were built as stur-dily as the first construction he'd encountered in this world. Using the window ledges and lintels, Maurice began to climb.

He spread his weight as wide as he could while tra-versing the roof. The front of the tenement was below him now. Yes, he'd positioned himself correctly. With luck, approaching from above, he could achieve the el-ement of surprise.

A susurrus went through the assembled onlookers as Maurice came over the cornice of the building. They began pointing.

What was wrong with these people? Maurice won-dered. Did they want the woman to get killed?

Descending the building facade was considerably more difficult than the climb. And the crowd kept get-ting louder. The hostage-taker must inevitably look up, see him . . .

Maurice tried to hurry. His foot slipped. At the same moment, a gust of wind came down from the river, bil-lowing his cape, tearing at him.

Another element in the stew of emotions bom-barding him suddenly came to the fore. It was the anticipation he'd noted earlier. The feeling was concen-trated below him, reaching a climax.

As surely as if he had heard it, he sensed someone giving a command: "Now."

Maurice couldn't zero in any further. His cape, swol-len with the breeze like the sail of a ship, tore him from his finger- and toe-holds. He was peeled away from the side of the building and dropped like a stone, instinctively shifting mental strength to his aura.

Thus, his telekinetic field was at its fullest power as Maurice tumbled to the street below—right into the field of fire of Antony Carron's gunmen hidden on the first floor.

He landed sideways as a snarling storm of automatic gunfire erupted from the ground-floor windows. The MAC-10 bullets should have torn through the police, riddled the bystanders, and created an ugly picture of the aftermath of ill-advised giant interference.

Instead, the gunfire struck the recumbent form of Maurice.

Searing pain ran up Maurice's left arm. He'd just suffered the worst injury one of his kind could receive: a broken bone. Jarred and half-stunned from his fall, he somehow maintained a semblance of shielding. Gunshots hammered at him, hard enough for him to feel the impacts. He threw a searching thought to the apartment above. The woman lived. The gunman upstairs had withdrawn after luring Maurice in.

Behind him, the street crowd surged like a mindless animal intent on flight, while a few of the police attempted to return fire.

Maurice forced himself up one-handed to his knees. He crawled forward, drawing most of the would-be assassins' fire. Bullets spanged around him. His cape, unprotected by his aura, was torn to ribbons.

He reached the stoop of the house. Lurching first left, then right, he reached in through the shattered parlor windows. Each time, the giant grabbed a gunman and hurled him backhanded into the street, letting him fall where he might.

The firing ceased, and police stormed the tenement. Right behind them came the charge of the media. Most of the camera crews stopped at the building's stoop, where Maurice lay slumped in agony.

". . . a true Hero, not only resolving the hostage crisis, but averting a bloodbath from hidden snipers. Maurice, how are you feeling?"

The cameraman was zooming in on Maurice's pale, sweaty face. But the reporter realized the giant's left arm was hanging at an unnatural angle. "He's been hurt! Get the paramedics over here!"

Seconds later, Maurice felt new twinges of pain as green-uniformed Lessers swarmed around his broken limb. One team seized his elbow, the other, his wrist, and they began pulling as if they were playing tug-of-war. The ends of the broken bone grated together. Maurice groaned, too weak to stop them.

"Don't worry," one of the medical workers assured him. "We'll get this set." The man frowned for a moment in perplexity. "Although, I don't know what we'll use for a splint."

Maurice stared muzzily down at the Lessers attending him.

They're helping me, he thought. *I guess they must like me.*

Then he descended into unconsciousness.

In the Grand Central Station of John Cameron's mind, Harry Sturdley paced back and forth, his resonating footsteps filling the air.

After what felt like a two-hour wait, Sturdley had

glanced at his watch to find that only fifteen minutes had elapsed. Several hours had passed since then, and Harry suspected he had paced off the distance from New York to Buffalo.

John Cameron had simply leaned against one of the walls, keeping unnaturally still the whole time. Sturdley had strictly refrained from disturbing him. Distraction here might mean an eternal fall through the Rift.

Now, however, Cameron stirred. "It's time," he said.

Sturdley stood at his new protege's side and closed his eyes. The gut-twisting sense of the Rift passed over them.

He opened his eyes to see a procession emerging up the ramp.

Robert led the way, leading a heroic but somewhat bruised figure. "There is turbulence back home," Robert explained quickly. "These people were glad to leave." He indicated his bruised friend. "This is Thomas."

The first impression Sturdley got of the oncoming new giant was of the tremendously toned abdominal muscles. The guy had Murphy Anderson abdominals, Harry thought. Only Anderson could draw muscles like that. Thomas, however, was a living, breathing rendition of those perfectly defined lines.

Over Robert's shoulder, Sturdley saw the face of a beautiful woman—his first giantess. Robert must have caught the thought. "And this is Barbara."

She stepped forward, revealing an amazonian body to go with the knockout face. Barbara moved with a lithe grace that was breathtaking.

Sturdley's mouth was already wide open. No one had

told him that female giants wore as much—or rather as little—clothing as the men.

He tried to tear his eyes away from the beautifully curved, beautifully tanned breasts. "My God," he hissed, "those are large enough to sit on!"

Happy Harry turned to John Cameron, who was now surrounded by expatriate giants.

"Kid," Sturdley said, "when you beam us home, make sure you take us to that isolated estate in Westchester. If we wind up in Central Park, the Comics Code will crucify us!"

He let his eyes turn in Barbara's direction again. "She has *got* to have her own book," Sturdley said. "Just as soon as we give her a costume!"

Harry turned to John. "Will moving more of them be a problem?"

John shook his head.

"Then let's get going," Sturdley said. "We've got new worlds to conquer."

Robert smiled as he marshaled his people.

CHAPTER 16

As Sturdley opened his eyes and threw off the vertigo of his latest jaunt through the Rift, he found himself facing a good-sized stone house surrounded by trees. This must be the Westchester estate the Fantasy Factory had leased as a home for the Heroes. At least, he hoped so. Harry had no way of knowing how John Cameron handled the spatial aspect of these jumps through nothingness. What if he'd landed them in the wrong place? How would the householders react to the spectacle of nearly fifty oversized trespassers, half of them buxom half-clad giantesses?

It was full dark, and there were lights in the windows. Sturdley motioned for his charges to stay back in the darkness as he went to knock on the front door. Relief nearly overwhelmed him when Frank McManus answered.

"You have anybody else here?" Harry immediately answered.

"No," the lawyer answered. "I figured we'd want to keep this—oh, my God."

He was staring over Sturdley's shoulder. Harry turned to see Barbara standing in the swathe of light coming from the doorway. It seemed to highlight her most salient features.

"Do all the giant women dress that way?" McManus asked. His eyes were the biggest Sturdley had ever seen.

"'Fraid so, Frank."

"We've got to figure out some way to cover them up. I mean, this is a reasonably isolated location, but people will be passing by. If they see those—those—"

"Yeah. She'll sell millions of comics for us once we get her covered up," Sturdley said. "I've been thinking about the problem since we got out of the Rift."

"Saul Marranais will never be able to run off twenty-five tops by tomorrow morning." McManus was nearly babbling.

"So, we'll have to improvise. I'm sure there are airports near here—commuter planes, maybe sky-diving schools."

"I'm not following you, Harry." The lawyer was looking at his boss as if Harry had lost his mind.

"Parachutes," Sturdley said. "We'll pay a premium price for twenty-five parachutes. Cut a hole in the top. I don't care what you call it—a caftan, poncho, or muumuu—it'll provide modesty for the time being."

Before Harry had finished, McManus was already heading for the Yellow Pages.

It took time, effort, and vast amounts of the Sturdley charm, but before midnight, several truckloads of parachutes had been trucked to the estate. McManus took delivery while Harry, Robert, and John herded the giants behind the house.

"I don't want anyone seeing your people until we're ready," Sturdley said.

The humans opened the packs while the giants unfurled the parachute canopies. Armed with kitchen knives that seemed ridiculously petite in their oversized hands, the giants worked to cut the cords. Sturdley and John, using the only two scissors they could find in the house, took on the delicate work, cutting head-sized holes in the center of the nylon shrouds.

It was sunrise by the time they'd finished. The female contingent stood in ranks, each giantess modestly arrayed in a huge white swath worn either straight down or tied around the waist.

"What do you think?" Sturdley said critically, taking in the effect.

"It looks like the world's tallest gospel choir," McManus said, looking a little stunned.

With daylight, the giants were setting out to explore their new domain. Males and females congregated on different parts of the lake shore. Unconcernedly, Barbara shucked her new gown and clout and dove into the water. This immediately initiated a round of skinny-dipping.

Harry's eyes sought the sky. "Let's hope we're off the general flight paths," he said tiredly. "We've got a lot to teach these people before we let them out in public."

By afternoon, the first Fantasy Factory staffers had arrived for the crash orientation project. Diane Jessup and Yvette Zelcere arrived to teach the female contingent deportment, for want of a better word—the dos and taboos of life in New York City. The urbane and much-traveled Elvio Vital was to tackle the same subject with the males, aided by Maurice, who would be taking some well-deserved recovery leave.

News of Maurice's heroic action had reached Westchester in the midst of the impromptu tailoring stint. Sturdley had big plans. "I've got a bidding war going on for the advertising rights on his sling. Right now, the top contenders are Coke, Nike, and 'After this, I'm going to Disneyworld,'" Harry boasted.

Maurice arrived in another Sturdley innovation. Rather than having John beam him in via the Rift, Harry had the giant delivered by moving van.

"We've got a licensing deal with Atlas Van Lines," Frank McManus explained to John. "They'll get recognition as the official transportation of the heroes, and the giants will be able to move around with less crowds getting in the way."

"If it works out, we'll call the special vans Heromobiles," Harry said as the truck pulled up.

The driver opened the back doors, and Maurice got out somewhat awkwardly, using only one hand. He looked a little dazed, but pleased. "They *like* me," he told Robert with a silly grin on his face. "It was just an accident that I saved them all. I fell in the right place. Then they fixed my arm."

He gestured to the chest. That's when Sturdley finally realized what the big blue sling represented—the remains of his precious cape. He let out a yell of protest, until Maurice explained that the cape was the reason he'd fallen in the first place.

"All right," he said, recognizing defeat. "No more capes. At least that should make Marranais happy."

"Nothing will make Marranais happy," Frank McManus said. "He's still trying to cope with an order for twenty-five giant women's spandex tops that don't need built-in support but do need to hide the merchandise."

In any event, Sturdley couldn't stay angry at Maurice for too long. Although he'd always considered him the second-string hero, Maurice's incredible rescue on 181st Street had led to a landslide of popular support for the giants, especially when it was discovered that the attack had been set up by the czar of New York's biggest gun-running ring. That operation was smashed, and its boss was now a hunted fugitive. Aside from an extortionate paramedic bill, the episode had been a big plus.

Another arrival had hitched a ride up on the truck: Val Innozenzio, a veteran Fantasy Factory writer and illustrator. Sturdley intended to use his expertise to teach crucial course: the ins and outs of the Comics Code. "We were lax with Robert and Maurice," Harry declared. "This bunch will be indoctrinated right from the beginning. Lesson One: no skinny-dipping."

Peg Faber also arrived to take over the administrative end of things. Her gray eyes were larger than usual as she took in the giants who would be her charges for the next few weeks, and she looked searchingly at John Cameron.

"I guess you don't need me now," the kid said, apparently eager to get away from the giants now that he had delivered them. "I guess I'll head back to the office." He glanced a little uncertainly at Sturdley. "Uh—do you want a lift?"

"Excellent idea," Harry said. "Cut out a lot of commuting time and let me hit the ground running."

"Yes," Peg agreed. "John will be very busy, too."

Sturdley turned, a little baffled by her tone of voice. "What?"

"I heard what you promised John if he'd bring the giants over." Pam's voice was very firm. "You said he could draw the new book with Robert as the hero."

"I didn't—" Sturdley began, then stopped to reconsider. Had he made some sort of rash promise in the heat of the moment?

"You said you would make him a star," Peg pointed out, prodding his memory. "That it would be his dream come true."

That had a horribly familiar ring. "You don't really mean to hold me to that, do you kid?" Sturdley turned to John, who was staring at Peg with awe on his face.

"Well, gee . . ." John Cameron stumbled like a little kid forced to recite for class. "I don't know . . ."

"I do." Peg was now aiming a glare at Sturdley. "Happy Harry Sturdley's word is his bond. You'd never say something you didn't *mean*, would you, Harry?"

Caught between the kid's hero-worship and his assistant's hard words, Sturdley said nothing.

"You take Mr. Sturdley back to his office," Peg ordered, taking charge. "Then go back to your room. I called the Putniks as soon as you turned up. There's also a check waiting for you at reception to pay your rent. Get your art samples back to the office and show them to Mr. Sturdley."

"Oh—okay!" John said. He grabbed Harry by the shoulder. Vertigo immediately overtook them, and the fall into emptiness was more like a dive-bomber's descent.

Harry appeared in his office, and John Cameron

winked out of existence. They'd never gone through the Rift so quickly before.

Marty Burke was on Park Avenue, right outside the offices of the Fantasy Factory. But the scene was somehow all *wrong*. Burke felt as though he were looking through a wide-angle lens. The street itself was wider than it should be, while the tops of the buildings all seemed to point toward each other under an impossibly blue sky. Forced perspective—that's what it was, he realized. It's the kind of view I always use in Mr. Pain.

If Burke needed any more proof, it came from the thunderous voice filling the air overhead. "It's an all-new Fantasy Factory team-up!" the reverberating voice said. "Featuring the Sensational Six and Mr. Pain!"

When Marty brought his eyes down to street level again, he saw a skirmish line of costumed heroes stretched across the avenue.

"Don't worry, Mr. Burke." Marty recognized Bob Bulrush, aka Dr. Rush, the leader of the Sensational Six in his purple full-face mask and dove-gray unitard. "We won't let them get through to you!"

"Don't sweat it, Marty-baby," another voice brashly announced. Burke turned to see Mr. Pain in his usual black-and-blue costume. The hero grinned and continued, "We're the best heroes in the business. And when you've got the best, you don't sweat the rest."

A little vein began to beat in Burke's temple. Not only did the character talk with Thibault dialogue, he was speaking in the whiny bastard's voice!

"Heads up!" Jumboy cried in warning. "Here they come!"

Park Avenue began to shake with the rumble of

heavy footsteps approaching from a sidestreet. The afternoon sun threw vast, misshapen shadows onto the pavement, and finally the antagonists came into view.

Burke recognized them immediately: Robert and Maurice.

"It's butt-kicking time!" Jumboy shouted joyfully, swelling up to his full twenty-foot height as he moved to take on Maurice. But the giant got in the first move, a vicious kick to the groin that knocked Jumboy to the street.

"Not Code! Not Code!" Jumboy moaned, writhing on the ground as Maurice proceeded to kick him repeatedly, then stomped his head until it was reduced to jelly.

"Noooooooo!" Jumboy's sister, Waterwoman, leapt forward with a scream. Every fire hydrant on the block erupted, creating a huge waterspout that struck Maurice on the chest. It had about as much effect on him as a water pistol. The Maid of Mists was pulling herself together for another attack when Robert stepped forward, his gigantic foot landing on her before she could change to her aqueous form. He crushed her down, stomping, crushing, until the knee-deep water in the street was tinged with red.

"We're not working as a team!" raged Dr. Rush. "Pain, you and I will distract the blond beast while Dark Matter and Hotbreath deal with the dark-haired giant."

Dr. Rush streaked toward Robert so fast, he was actually running atop the water on the street. Burke's favorite superhero fired a rocket-piton into the face of a building across the avenue and swung up toward the giant's face.

Meanwhile, Dark Matter made his ponderous way toward Maurice. Inside the blocky, black mass of his body, a spiral galaxy began pinwheeling inward. "We gonna mess you up, buddy," he said, his face as grim as a cruel god carved in ebony. "I'm gonna hold you down while my partner gives you a hotfoot all over!"

The stars congealed down into a single black point as Dark Matter exerted his gravitic powers, aiming to crush Robert where he stood. The blond giant stumbled as the pull on him increased. His shoulder brushed a building, then his hand struggled up, shattering an office window and flinging a desk at Dark Matter. Drawn by the superhero's gravitic pull, it smashed into his chest, knocking him flat.

Robert then flashed into action, stooping to seize Hotbreath and lifting him as if he were a baby. The seven-foot-tall dragon thrashed his tail and tried to turn his face to blast the giant with his fiery breath, but Robert held him away, hands on either side of the dragon's chest.

Then the hands began squeezing. Hotbreath writhed and struggled—then something went *crunch* within his chest.

Raging mad, Dr. Rush dashed straight for Maurice, intending to use his momentum to run right up the giant's body. The dark-haired giant stood still, gauging his time, then stomped out with inhuman reflexes. The water on the street grew pinker as more blood was added.

That left Mr. Pain, swinging on his line in a kamikaze attack at Maurice's face. The giant brought up both fists in a double hammer-blow, smashing the hero out of the air. Mr. Pain pinwheeled through the air to land with a sickening thud at Burke's feet.

"Didn't feel a thing," he gasped, blood pouring from his grinning mouth. Behind his mask, his eyes were going glassy. "Which is more than I can say for you."

Marty Burke looked up to see that the giants had almost reached him. Both raised their feet, then brought them down on him . . .

Burke shuddered upright, the tendons in his throat and neck pulled so tight they burned. He stared down at the drawing board in front of him, one set of images smeared from where his face had rested. He'd been pulling an all-nighter, roughing out a Mr. Pain story to replace the abomination Thibault had tried to stick him with.

"Must have dropped off," he groaned, forcing himself to his feet. "That was a hell of a dream."

Burke stumbled to the coffeemaker, emptied the last cup from the pot, and headed to the bathroom. The face in the mirror staring blearily at him was disheveled and stubble-faced. A blurry pencil image of Mr. Pain had transferred itself to his right cheek. Burke washed it off, splashing cold water in his face. He took a gulp of cold coffee, his stomach roiling from the stale brew, and headed back to the drawing board.

"Who is it?" Burke snarled as the buzzer sounded in his studio. His manner changed when Thad Westmoreland's voice came over the annunciator system. It could be useful if his editor gave a quick blessing to the new story and saved him some precious time.

But Westmoreland had obviously not come over to discuss the latest comic script. "Sturdley is up to something," the cadaverous editor announced when he came in the door. "He's been holed up someplace in Westchester all night, and today a lot of the staff hasn't shown up at the office. Especially some of the old guys—Innozenzio and Vital."

Burke frowned. "What can he be doing? Setting up a Fantasy Factory old-age home?"

"Or a giant hero training-ground," Westmoreland said. "They moved Maurice up there after he got winged last night." He looked around the studio, littered as it was with crumpled paper and cigarette butts. "Did you hear about what happened?"

"I caught a rerun of the news at about one in the morning," Burke said. He'd noticed that Leslie Ann Nasotrudere had been noticeably absent from the *First News* reports lately. "So what do you think? Sturdley's giving his pet giants remedial training?"

"I don't *know*!" Westmoreland burst out. "I can tell you this, though. Somehow Sturdley got into his office without anyone seeing him. He nearly gave Zeb Grantfield a heart attack, since Zeb was sitting at Faber's desk when Sturdley came out."

"So?"

"Sturdley asked Zeb how the practice on drawing giants was turning out. He wondered how a giant female would look."

Burke smashed a fist down on his drawing board. "I *knew* that bastard would try to get to Grantfield! And sure enough, Grantfield is cozying up to Sturdley behind our backs. Somebody should take that kid down a peg or two. He thinks he's the greatest thing since . . ."

Seeing the look on Westmoreland's face, Burke let his tirade run down.

"You know," Thad Westmoreland said, "for a second, you sounded just like Sturdley."

Burke ignored the comment, his mind focusing on another aspect of the puzzle. "Sturdley's got an isolated estate up in Westchester, his pet giants, a training course—and he's hinting about a book with a giant superheroine." He pushed his hair back with one hand. "Suppose he's got himself a giantess up there?"

"From where?" Westmoreland asked.

Burke shrugged. "From wherever he got the other two."

"Great!" Westmoreland's bony face got even tighter. "Then he's got another sure-selling book to beat us over the head with."

Marty Burke listened to Westmoreland rant with only half an ear. He just realized that he had something—a little news tip to drop in Leslie Ann's ear.

Harry Sturdley leaned back in his executive chair, a cat-who-ate-the-canary smile on his face. He had just seen some amazingly good art from two unexpected sources. First, thanks to Peg Faber's blackmail, he'd looked at what John Cameron could do. When the kid came in with his illustrations, Harry had already prepared a little speech to let him down gently. But the words had died on his lips as he looked at the pictures.

Incredibly, John Cameron had real talent. Oh, he was a little raw and would need direction, but he had what it took to be a star. The only way Sturdley could explain it was that there was a weird mental quirk at work, like those guys who could do complex math equations in their heads but couldn't tie their own shoes. He'd checked his medical library for the actual term: the idiot savant syndrome.

It seemed that no sooner had he sent John and his art off to Bob Gunnar than Zeb Grantfield came in. The wonderkid also had some illustration board under his arm. "Harry," he said hesitantly, "remember when you asked me before how the giant thing was coming? Especially female giants?"

Sturdley nodded. So the ambitious little weasel was making a play already! This would do wonders for Marty Burke's blood pressure.

"I think you should look at these." Grantfield held out the illustrations.

Sturdley's eyes narrowed at the first picture: a big-busted, slim-hipped giantess shaking a gang of crooks out of a compact car. Then came a giant heroine punching in a window to get at a gunman. Last was a pure cheesecake shot: the giantess carrying a huge old Wurlitzer juke box the way most kids carried a boom box. The proportions were pure Grantfield, but the line, lithe and fluid, was not. And this heroine had pupils in her eyes.

"Who did this?" Harry asked.

Grantfield smiled. "Mack Nagel. You know, we've been working pretty closely. I guess he taught me a lot about layout. And it looks, well, like some of my style rubbed off on him."

Mack Nagel. Who'd have thought that after years of skinny horror-comic hosts, the old guy would turn out to have a genius for drawing giant women?

Sturdley kept the pictures, intending to show them to Bob Gunnar a little later. He wouldn't mind having another rabbit to pull out of his hat. Even editors-in-chief need a reason to respect the boss.

The phone rang, and Eddie Walcott, back on the desk outside, buzzed in. "It's Peg for you."

Sturdley picked up the phone in an expansive mood. "Everything going well up there?" he asked.

"Well enough." Peg sounded a bit constrained, though. "Harry, what's the idea of having everything the giants eat catered from MacBurgers?"

"That's the *Heroes*," Sturdley corrected her, "not *giants*. From here on in, that's how we refer to them."

"Right now, I'm more interested in this fast-food diet," Peg plowed on.

"It's cost effective, and they assured me it's better balanced than the deli food we've been giving Robert and Maurice. Best of all, it's *free*. MacBurgers has the license to do Hero Meals with a new giantburger, and officially approved likenesses on the packaging—"

"And you don't have to pay the feed bill," Peg finished. "Let me tell you, Mr. Pennysaver, the prototype Hero Meals did not sit well in all the Heroes' stomachs." She coughed. "And you do not know what it's like to be caught next to a twenty-foot-tall person with gas."

Barbara went lazily into a backstroke, enjoying the flow of water across her flesh. The early morning sun had barely risen above the pines on the hills overlooking the lake.

From the shore of the lake, Robert glared at her, his hands on his hips. Beside his feet lay an untidy balloon of nylon and Barbara's clout.

"You know the rule," he began in annoyance.

She turned to tread water. "Oh, yes, all the rules. Things to be done in secret, in the woods. Classes on how not to offend the feelings of the Lessers. Really, Robert, do you seriously intend to let this little Sturdley man rule our lives like this? I remember a very different man in the woods outside my father's holding."

"This is a different world, where we have much to learn before we can move. And Sturdley is a useful teacher. Now, get out of that water and into your—"

"That bag-thing?" Barbara laughed. "But I much prefer to bathe this way. At least this isn't a public park where someone can come running along—Maurice told me that story."

"I still want you out before someone sees you."

"Why do you worry so about what the Lessers think of us? Or is it concern for them?"

"It's not the Lessers. It's our own people. I set this rule, and all will obey it."

"All?" Barbara said in a provocative voice.

"All," Robert said flatly. "No one challenges my authority." He picked up the nylon shift. "I've just thought of a rather useful side to this. It would cover any bruises you might receive."

For a moment, Barbara continued silently treading water. Then she struck out for the shore.

Just as she rose out of the water, Robert stared across the lake, into the sun. "A flying machine."

"Where?" Barbara turned.

Robert's face tightened as his mental probe encountered a familiar mind. "There's a newsgatherer—an enemy. Get dressed and into the woods."

Barbara bent to get her clout. Robert kicked it into

the lake, thrusting the nylon poncho at her. "Just this. Go! Those machines are fast. This one will be on top of us soon."

Fumbling, Barbara pulled the poncho over herself, then ran for the shelter of the trees. She didn't need her immaterial senses to locate the machine now. She could hear the clatter of its engine as it swooped down over the lake.

"Now perhaps you see that Sturdley and his rules have uses," Robert called mockingly after her.

Leslie Ann Nasotrudere snarled a malediction. "Did you get anything?" she asked her cameraman.

Angie shook his head. "We were too far away, even for a telephoto lens. It's like they knew we were coming before we got in range."

Those blasted freak-senses again, Leslie Ann thought, glaring down at the blond-haired giant. "So we've got sweet nothing—"

A now very-familiar figure, one arm in a sling embroidered with advertising, came walking into the clearing—from the opposite direction that the first giant figure had run!

"Three of them," Leslie Ann said in satisfaction. "Three of them, where there used to be two. Hey!" she yelled to the chopper pilot, "take us home. We've got our scoop."

CHAPTER 17

When the "three giants" tape aired on *First News*, Sturdley reluctantly had to take the wraps off his training camp for heroes. Still, he managed to introduce the place in his best marketing fashion. His two proven-quality heroes, Robert and Maurice, took the press on a tour of the place, and only select new giants, well-coached, actually appeared on camera.

Saul Marranais kept threatening to disappear on a long cruise, but he did come through with more costumes, both male and female. As soon as she was covered up in the new unitard, Barbara was presented to the public. So was the redheaded Thomas with his impressive muscular development, and a redheaded giantess named Ruth.

Public opinion was high on the idea of more giants making the streets safer, so Sturdley figured he'd come through the latest crisis well ahead of the game.

Still, there was one unexpected result. After the coverage on the estate came out, Sturdley got an angry phone call from Saul Marranais.

"I don't know what you've got to complain about," Harry said into the phone. "We gave you full credit for the costumes the heroes were wearing."

"Yeah? What about those poncho things most of the giant women were wearing?" Marranais said in tones of deep annoyance.

"Saul, those were emergency improvisations. We had to cover up the Heroines with *something*."

"Well, I wish you'd told me about it," Saul Marranais huffed. "One of my competitors saw them on TV and knocked off a whole line of them in different shades of nylon. He's calling it the Giant Look, and the ponchos are selling like hotcakes."

Sturdley's only response was a sigh. Who could figure the vagaries of fashion?

Happy Harry also took an evil pleasure in the Fantasy Factory's next staff meeting. For one thing, the Burke-Westmoreland axis was suddenly reduced to a minor cog in the company machine, overshadowed by the excitement over doing the giant books. Not even *The Death of the Glamazon* could compete with a book of real-life Hero adventures.

In fact, the alliance between Burke and Westmoreland nearly fell apart altogether when Thad Westmoreland got a look at the first few pages of Robert's adventures. The cadaverous little editor's eyes had blazed with paranoia as he glared at Sturdley. "It's not enough that you stick Marty with *Mr. Pain*, the Glamazon project, and *Latter-Day Breed*. Now you've got him working on your giant books, too?"

Westmoreland directed a "why didn't you tell me

about this?" look to Burke, who in turn seemed a little green about the gills as he stared at the artwork.

"This stuff isn't Marty's," Sturdley assured the upset editor. "It's a new artist, under exclusive contract to draw the Robert book."

"You're sure it's not Burke?" Zeb Grantfield said, looking over the pages. "I was going to say this is some of the best stuff I'd seen him do in ages."

"No, it's a different guy completely—although you do know him," Sturdley said, enjoying the moment.

"Who?" Marty Burke asked in a dull voice.

Happy Harry smiled. "John Cameron."

Zeb Grantfield stared in astonishment, and maybe a little professional jealousy. "You mean the kid?" he asked.

"Yup," Sturdley said, rubbing their noses in it. "Not only is he fast, but he draws from memory—no photo reference necessary. Isn't it amazing how he gets such perfect likenesses of Robert and Maurice?"

It was a moment to savor, as was the staff's reaction when Harry showed them Mack Nagel's art for the Barbara book. Okay, so Mack needed photos of Barbara to get the face right, but everyone was impressed with what Kyle Everard called "the Grantfield fusion" style.

And Nagel had put pupils in the characters' eyes.

Sturdley enjoyed his triumph. It was quite pleasant to have people considering him a comics genius again.

But there was a completely unexpected complication for the hero comics. Bob Gunner brought it up. "The problem with real heroes," he said, "is that they've got real names—and just first names, at that. I've been trying to come up with titles, and frankly, I'm stuck. If we just call a book *Heroes*, it sounds too generic."

Elvio Vital had smiled. "Well, once a year you can put out a Giant Annual."

"That doesn't help us for the other eleven months," Sturdley said, ignoring the joke. "We've got two heroes, and two books. What are we going to call them?"

"Happy Harry Sturdley stuck for a name?" Thad Westmoreland drawled, trying to go on the attack again. "Why not call them *Harry's Heroes*? or even better, *The Amazing Robert* and *The Fantastic Barbara*?"

A slow smile had crept over Harry's face. "You think those titles are too stupid to sell? We'll see."

A week after the books were announced and offered to the nation's comics shops, Bob Gunnar burst into Sturdley's office nearly tearing his hair out with excitement. "Yvette Zelcere just called me with ballpark figures on *The Amazing Robert* and *The Fantastic Barbara*," he gloated. "Looks like we'll top five million copies each, pre-sold! And Dynasty thought they were making sales history with *Farewell, Zenith—The Death of the Man of Molybdenum*! We've left that in the shade!"

"Circulate a memo with the good news," Sturdley said, rubbing his hands together, "with a special copy for Thad Westmoreland."

Interestingly, although the comics world hailed the appearance of the Heroes books in the Fantasy Factory galaxy, Sturdley faced headaches in the real world. The media threatened an anti-Hero backlash as the news came out, with several commentators attacking the company, and Sturdley, for putting the Heroes into costumes.

Happy Harry called an impromptu press conference,

featuring before and after photographs of Robert and Maurice, and what he later considered his all-time best sound bite: "I just don't understand the problem over the costumes. To my knowledge, this is the first time comics have been criticized for putting clothes *on* heroes."

But Sturdley wasn't the only one to face dissension over his plans. Up in Westchester, a group of heroes-in-training confronted Robert.

"How long are we supposed to endure these Lessers telling us what to do?" Thomas burst out. "They cover us up in these second skins, play the part of teachers, and expect us to abide by this nonsensical code that only exists for imaginary beings!"

The red-haired giant thrust his face at Robert. "This is not what you promised us when you came to the main holding. Where are our domains? Where are our Lessers? Oh, certainly the little ones idolize *you*. I saw you on the magic box—the television—with the one called Oprah. They all applaud and kiss up to you. But what about the rest of us? We're left here to work like Lessers, and expected to treat Lessers as though they were our Masters!"

Robert moved fast. The first intimation any of the dissidents had of the blow was the red mark on Thomas' face. It was delivered with enough force to knock the surprised giant down.

Impassive, Robert stood over him, forcing a mental probe through Thomas' disordered shields. "Remember well who I am before you take that tone with me. And remember too that any comments about our long-range plans are to be made mind-to-mind."

Robert's scathing glance took in all the dissidents—

Victor and Quentin, Ida, Ruth, and Eve. "All you have shown me is that you still have much to learn about this world. And it's just as well that the Lessers be your teachers. These aren't the Lessers we knew on our world. These ones are wild, conditioned to think of themselves as free. They have weapons—"

"I've seen their precious guns," Victor cut in. "In practice, their projectiles barely impinge on my shields."

"But you haven't encountered bombs," Robert returned. "Or the things they call A-bombs, that can destroy entire cities. Are you so sure your shields could survive *that*?"

He looked around at the circle of faces following his mental argument. "The Lessers of this world are unused to our control. So first we must make them love us—*then* we can guide them. Finally—"

"Why can't we let them be?"

The mental query came from beyond the edge of the group, from the one who was smallest in size—Gideon.

"The humans have developed rather admirably on their own," Gideon thought. "You've obviously read about their weapons. But I've been reading about their laws, their ideas of personal freedom. We could learn—"

His discourse was terminated by the conjoined hatred and disgust of the others.

"Just what I would expect from a weakling." Victor's dislike filled the mental waves like a cloud.

"A defective who should never have reached this age," Thomas thought.

"Who'd mate with one like that?" Ida wanted to know.

Only Robert chose to dignify Gideon's thoughts with a logical response, and that was more because the choice to bring Gideon to this world reflected on his leadership.

"Gideon, you come from a little woods-holding, at the very edge of the old Master's domain." Robert hesitated for a moment, searching for the correct argument. "Doubtless you had very few Lessers available, and so they were valuable to you. The others here, including myself, had many more of them. Here in this city alone, there are a good ten million of them. As you learn about the Lessers here, remember one thing. Lessers are cheap. They themselves value their lives cheaply, as you'll find when you confront their criminals. I receive the impression that you want to help them. So do we all."

Robert's thoughts bored into Gideon's brain. "We can give them order, meaning, value. Our guidance, our dominion, will give them value. Value to *us*."

"We in the PBA can understand the attraction of these vigilantes in their colorful costumes, offering a quick fix. But—" The police union spokesman broke from his prepared text. "Leslie Ann," he blurted in frustration, "we called this press conference for all the media. Why are you the only one here?"

"Cut," she said to Angie, her cameraman, a frown sharpening her Barbie-Doll features. Turning to the spokesman, she shook her head. "Ray, you've got to understand something. You haven't said anything new in the last five releases you've churned out. We already know you don't like costumed vigilantes. But Sturdley and his Hero factory up in Westchester keep churning them out. He's got more than twenty of them trained and walking the streets now. You can't keep playing the same old record."

"We thought of asking what stake they've got in the city," the PBA man said. "But hell, that raises the whole residency-requirement can of worms. I live in Suffolk, myself."

"Well you'd better come up with something," Leslie Ann Nasotrudere warned him.

"But what?" the spokesman moaned.

"It's not up to me to make the news," Nasotrudere said. Bitterly, she reflected that even though she'd broken the extra giants story, she'd wound up covering more flower and dog shows lately than real news. "But think about this. By the giants' own admission, they don't come from this world. What does that make them?"

"Freaks," the police spokesman responded immediately. "Aliens." He paused for a second, as if he were tasting the word in his mouth. "*Illegal* aliens."

"Mr. Sturdley," Ted Snopes of ICU News said, aiming his microphone at Happy Harry, "would you care to comment on the latest actions by the New York Patrolmen's Benevolent Association—the action brought in Federal court today to declare the Heroes illegal aliens?"

"Frankly, Ted," Harry responded, "I think the PBA had a better case when they tried to go after Robert and Maurice as vagrants when they were living in Central Park."

That had been a wonderful media mess, with all sorts of advocate groups for the homeless getting in on the act. The frantic efforts of the cops' union had been an almost ironic piece of life imitating comic art. Several Fantasy Factory books used police noncooperation as subplot material.

"Since Robert, Maurice, and the other Heroes now have a legal residence in Westchester and pay taxes on their book royalties, I don't see what the problem is. They provide a valuable service to the community."

Sturdley shook his head. "I wish I could decide what they were afraid of," he said to the thicket of microphones being aimed at him. "I'm not sure if the cops are worried about keeping their jobs or worried about keeping their guns. My answer to the first is we'll always need cops. My answer to the second is that they'd better talk to the department psychologist."

Things were finally settling down at the Fantasy Factory. The monthly issues of *The Amazing Robert* and *The Fantastic Barbara* were in production, and the indoctrination of the Heroes had been pretty much finished. The staffers who'd been up in Westchester had now returned to the office.

Sturdley was glad of that, especially glad to retire Eddie Walcott from the assistant's desk and welcome Peg Faber back. At first he hadn't noticed any difference in Peg, but it slowly began to dawn on him that she'd changed her style of dress. All of a sudden, her jeans disappeared and she was wearing skirts—short ones. Then she took to sleeveless tops. The toll on the art staff was considerable, and Sturdley gleefully hovered in his office doorway, pouncing to chastise all would-be suitors who were behind on their deadlines.,

Harry assumed that the object of Peg's affection was

the quick-drawing, smooth-talking Elvio Vital, and wished she'd listened more carefully to his advice before they'd set off for West Virginia. One day he saw her brighten and wave down the hall. He leaned out his door, expecting to see Elvio.

Instead, he found John Cameron bopping along, a sheaf of new illustrations under his arm and a big, goofy smile on his face.

Oh, Peg, no, Harry thought. *Please, anyone but him.* He beat a retreat into his office, a bewildered man.

The big day finally came—the official publication date for the first Heroes comics.

Sturdley stared expansively around the freshly cleaned space of the Fantasy Factory's bullpen. All work in progress had been locked away to protect it from this afternoon's cocktail party. Staff, press, and selected guests were celebrating an important comic book launch—one that wouldn't have been possible without Harry and John.

"Well, kid, we've made it," he said, turning to his new art discovery.

They were a study in contrast: Sturdley lean and perfectly tailored, John Cameron in jeans and a corduroy jacket that looked a size too small. But John was considerably less rumpled than usual. Somebody had even trimmed his hair.

Mack Nagel was in the crowd, looking considerably less threadbare in a new suit. Scattered here and there in the crowd, Sturdley noticed several woman sporting the "giant look."

The heroes were riding high. The latest federal statistics had come out yesterday, showing that hardly any guns were now making their way into New York City.

Robert and his corps of trainees were spreading the net of Hero protection over the greater metropolitan area. They'd already discovered it was a lot easier to interdict shipments of illegal guns on the Jersey Turnpike instead of the bridges and tunnels that fed into Manhattan.

Robert was an accredited celebrity, having made an appearance—al fresco—on *Donahue*.

Sturdley glanced at his watch. His head Hero was late. He had one of the office gofers stationed by his window, waiting for Robert to appear. That would signal the beginning of the press conference; then he could really get down to having a good time.

Harry looked around at the people filling the room. This wasn't just a celebration for the Fantasy Factory staff and a feature opportunity for the media. There were a lot of businessmen in attendance as well—potential licensers of Hero products. With an infusion of cash from them, the Fantasy Factory's shareholders would be happy indeed with the new comics line. The heroes' share of the profits would probably be enough to get them a Manhattan headquarters, if they could find a place with enough headroom.

"What do you think, son?" Sturdley asked, outlining his plans to his latest protege.

John Cameron looked uncomfortable. Sturdley had put that down to facing a roomful of people asking him questions and having to wear a tie. Now, though, the kid showed he had something on his mind. "I just don't know if it's a good idea to depend on the—the Heroes."

Sturdley noticed that John kept tripping over the Fantasy Factory's nomenclature for the giants.

"I don't know what your problem is, kid. The heroes are going to make you famous—and rich. You get a piece of the action, after all."

"I'm worried about *their* actions, Mr. Sturdley," John said. "I know you think you're running the deal with them, but *are* you?"

"We have a contract, kid," Sturdley reminded him.

That only made John Cameron look gloomier. "I just hope that's enough."

"It's enough for me," Sturdley assured him. He smiled. "Look, there's Burke and his pal Westmoreland. They look *sick* over this."

Marty Burke closed his eyes. His head was pounding horribly, his right temple felt as if it were about to burst, but he was not about to let Harry Sturdley push him out of the limelight. Cool liquid trickled down his palm. He opened his eyes to discover he'd gripped his plastic glass so tightly, it had cracked. Scotch on the rocks now dribbled across his hand. "Damn," Burke muttered. That was the third glass to go in the past hour.

"Take it easy, Marty," Thad Westmoreland said. "You've been pushing yourself too hard, juggling three projects at once. We'll probably reschedule the Glamazon thing, anyway, after this Hero hooplah subsides. Don't kill yourself. Get some sleep."

Burke only shuddered. "Sleep is the thing I want least of all," he said. "I keep having nightmares— dreams about those goddamn giants." He stared moodily at the blow-ups of John Cameron's art decorating the walls. "What do we know about them, really? They come from nowhere, take on an enormous, thankless job—why?"

Westmoreland laughed. "You sound like somebody from an old fifties sci-fi comic. 'If they're aliens, they gotta be evil.' Things have changed, Marty."

"Forgive me for butting in." Elvio Vital walked over to join the conversation. "But I have my doubts as well. In my country, one would wonder at the motives for such benevolence." He ran a hand over his eyes. "I've been having bad dreams, too."

Burke looked a little surprised. He and Elvio *never* agreed on anything.

Thad Westmoreland gave out a rasping laugh. "You two really had me going for a while there," the editor said. "What did you do, fix this up between yourselves? Nice bit. You should try it out on Sturdley."

Neither Burke nor Elvio said a word, and Westmoreland's laughter became more tentative. "I mean, it is a joke, isn't it? Whether we like it or not, these guys are making the company a lot of money. They've got a contract . . ."

He stumbled into an uneasy silence and drifted back into the party.

Sturdley glanced at his watch again, beginning to get annoyed. The van bringing Robert was supposed to have left Westchester an hour and a half ago. Where was his hero? He began making his way out of the bullpen, heading for his office. If the gofer on watch had screwed up, he'd—

"Nice party, Mr. Sturdley." Ted Snopes had a drink in one hand and a selection of canapes in the other. "But when are we getting to the press conference? A lot of people want to ask about last night's events."

"What events?" Sturdley asked, gauging his next move through the crowd.

"The armory break-ins, and the piles of weapons destroyed," Snopes said.

Harry stopped dead in his tracks. "What?"

"There was a puddle of motor oil in one of the vehicle docks," Snopes went on, giving Harry's face an eagle-like stare. "There was a partial footprint left on the scene—a three-foot long footprint. You can see why we'd like to talk with Robert.

"I mean, Robert has been complaining lately that the only guns on the street have been ripped off from armories. We'd like to know if this could be his way of cutting off that supply source."

"But—but—but—" Happy Harry took a deep breath. *Stop sounding like a motorboat,* he told himself. "That's federal property! The heroes would never—"

The crowd opened, and he saw John Cameron chatting with Peg Faber.

"Excuse me a second," Harry said, "there's someone I have to talk to."

"Lovely party, Harry," Peg said as he came over. She looked at John Cameron, and dimples appeared in her cheeks. "I really like your tie. I don't think I've ever seen you in one."

John turned bright red. "I had to ask Elvio to tie the knot for me," he confessed.

"Excuse me, young lovers," Sturdley interrupted, "but we've got a problem." He related Ted Snope's bombshell.

"Maybe that's why Robert hasn't shown," Peg said, frowning.

"We've got to find out where he is," Sturdley said,

staring at John. "Then you either Rift him in, or Rift me out there—"

A commotion at the entrance to the bullpen cut him off. Uniformed men suddenly appeared in the doorway.

"INS!" one of the men shouted as he held up his I.D. "We're here under the Immigration and Naturalization Act of 1987, which states that any company employing illegal aliens is subject to—"

"Well, I'll be damned," Sturdley said in a faint voice. "The PBA must have friends in high places."

Harry stepped forward. "Just what does this mean?" he demanded.

"It means you're under arrest, for employing undocumented aliens—namely, the giants." The federal agent's face was impassive. "All corporate assets will be frozen—"

"Wait a second!" one of the artists blurted out. "Assets frozen? I'm supposed to be getting a check—"

Angry Fantasy Factory workers clustered around the agent, bombarding him with questions and demands.

"Looks like we're in for a hell of a time," Harry said numbly.

"Only if they catch you." John Cameron suddenly flung one arm around Sturdley, the other around Peg. He took a deep breath, and his eyes lost focus.

The ground dropped from under them as they fell into an endless void.

CHAPTER 18

Harry opened his eyes to find himself in John Cameron's Grand Central Station of the mind.

"So that was the Rift," Peg said. She looked a little gray and shaky. "Where are we?"

"This is the Rift, too," John quickly explained. "We're sort of between worlds right now. I thought this would be the best place to go while Mr. Sturdley makes plans."

Happy Harry had to shake his head at the kid's belief that he could come up with a plan to get out of this mess. Of course, he'd *better* come up with a plan. Right now, he was a fugitive from federal justice. His company was accused of hiring illegal aliens—hell, he'd *imported* them.

What was the penalty for that? Harry didn't know, but he suspected it would be stiff.

"Okay," he said. "We'll have to approach this a couple of different ways. First is the legal problem. Frank McManus will go to work on that." He grimaced. "We might even need Ira Orreck."

Harry paused, struck by a thought. "I know that immigration is allowed by quota. But how do they set quotas for people from new nations—countries that didn't exist a year ago? Maybe there's a way we can play that. The Heroes are from a new country."

"A new world," Peg said.

"At least, it's a new one to us." Harry began to feel more confident. There were angles here, handles to be grabbed.

"Think Bushmiller," Harry said, half to himself.

"What?" Peg said.

"Ralph Waldo Bushmiller," Harry amplified.

"Oh, the publisher in *The Rambunctious Rodent*," John said. "What's he got to do with anything?"

"He's got to be our inspiration right now. In the comic, he's always getting into hot water over something the Rodent has pulled off. We're in a similar situation with the Heroes. So we've got to come up with a Bushmiller solution."

He frowned, deep in thought, then snapped his fingers. "We had a storyline where Bushmiller was all set for the chop, until he joined forces with the Rodent, getting the exclusive scoop on several incredible stories."

Harry looked at his dubious companions. "That's what we've got to do: rouse the heroes to do something so outstanding, public opinion will force all this nonsense to go away." A slow smile crossed his face. "I've got just the thing." He turned to Peg and John. "What would you say if, for twenty-four hours, Manhattan had a *zero* crime rate?"

"I'd say you could probably have yourself elected king," Peg responded.

"I'll settle for Get out of Jail Free," Sturdley said. "But this all depends on catching up with Robert. Where the hell would he be?"

"Maybe he's hashing out what happened at the armory with the other giants—and I know where they're *supposed* to be," Peg said. "We sent two tons of food up to the Westchester house."

"Okay. John, send me there, then you go back and talk to McManus. I'm going to have Robert turn me into INS—that'll get us some press coverage." Harry sighed. "After that, it will be up to the lawyers and the heroes."

Sturdley glanced around. "How do I get back?"

John pointed to a tunnel entrance that now read: "Westchester."

"Just start on down. I'll take care of the rest."

Sturdley started walking. It was fine and all to have someone with paranormal powers to locate the heroes' leader. But they should have a more normal way to call on Robert. Maybe signal flares, or a searchlight . . .

Happy Harry grimaced. If he got out of this mess, he'd have to look into some way of getting Hero-sized mobile phones.

In the middle of that thought, he felt a now-familiar sinking sensation. Instinctively, he closed his eyes. He opened them in bright sunlight on the rolling rear lawn of the Westchester retreat. A buffet table had been set up on the flagstone patio, but the giants were arranged in a circle on the grass, Robert sitting in the middle.

They seemed to be having some sort of argument, but not a word came from any of the fifty. Great, Sturdley thought. Fighting by telepathy.

Harry started walking toward them, and Robert

caught the movement. When the Heroes' leader saw him, a look of consternation clouded his face.

"What are you doing here?" Robert barked.

"Rift express," Harry said. "We've got big trouble. The federal government is after us, thanks to some political pressure—and this nonsense you've been pulling with the armories."

Robert's face froze. "Collections of weapons are too tempting to criminals."

"Forget that for now. We're fighting for our lives here. I see you've got all your people together. Good. Now we wait for a call. My lawyer should be talking to the press, then the cops. I'm on the run from the law right now, and you're going to turn me in."

The usually self-assured Robert gawked.

Harry explained their immigration problem and his fugitive status. "After turning me over with all the attendant media hoopla, you're going to make an announcement. For twenty-four hours, starting whenever I go into custody, the Heroes will be hitting the bricks to make the streets of Manhattan totally crime free." Harry smiled. "It will be a first in New York history."

Robert's golden eyebrows knit in thought. "You hope to sway public opinion."

"With luck, I'll be out of the hoosegow in one day, and we can get back to our real business."

The giant nodded. "Yes," he echoed, "our real business."

John and Peg returned to find the Fantasy Factory bullpen aswirl with people—and the Immigration agents quietly going nuts.

"Well, he was here a minute ago," Bob Gunnar said nervously to a red-faced INS official. "I saw him."

"Then where is he now?" the officer demanded.

"Did you try the men's room?" Peg boldly piped up. "I, ah, got the impression that's where he was headed when all this started."

Peg and John joined the crowd, whose decibel level had risen considerably. "We've got to hang together, people, until this gets sorted out," Bob Gunnar was saying.

"So speaks Sturdley's right-hand man," Thad Westmoreland yelled. "You may be representing a discredited regime, Gunnar. We'll see what the stockholders have to say about this."

Marty Burke said nothing, but Peg saw the calculating gleam in his eyes as he looked around the room. "It's starting already," she muttered. "Without Harry, this place will blow up."

There was an ugly shouting match, but Gunnar managed to assert his authority, ending the party and sending people back to their desks and drawing boards.

Peg and John moved to intercept Frank McManus. They drew him aside and passed along Sturdley's instructions. "So, I'm to arrange for a surrender in Westchester, with an attendant media circus." The lawyer nodded, sighed, and looked around him. "Harry sure throws one hell of a party."

An hour later, McManus had the surrender all arranged. It made a wonderful picture: stiff-backed federal officers taking Sturdley into custody against a backdrop of the entire hero force.

The remaining space on the front lawn of the

Westchester house was taken up by a vast media corps that included a triumphant Leslie Ann Nasotrudere, giving her own slant to the events her camera crew was recording.

"We, the Heroes, have an announcement to make." Robert's voice rumbled over the crowd, bringing all microphones to attention. "The actions today are clearly politically inspired, designed to make us look like criminals. We believe, however, that the American people know who the real criminals are, and which side we are on. My compatriots and I will protest Mr. Sturdley's arrest through our actions."

From the distance, a convoy of tractor-trailer moving vans came trundling up to the estate. "It is now three P.M.—the start of Operation Hero. For the next twenty-four hours, our full force will be on the streets of Manhattan, making it a no-crime zone. Hopefully, that will show what it means to have a city under hero protection—aliens or not."

Sturdley was marched off to one of the Immigration cars.

Well, he thought, *let's hope the big guys are up to it.*

CHAPTER 19

Peg Faber kept her head down, shuffling papers across her desk, listening to her radio through a single, tiny earphone.

She didn't want to see or talk to the people going up and down the corridor. This was always a busy office, but right now it was like Bloomingdale's in the middle of Christmas shopping season. Artists and assistants marched up and down the halls, singly and in groups, stopping in one editor's office and then going to see another. Gunnar and Westmoreland had seen most of the staff, while others snuck down the corridor to talk to Marty Burke. Peg wanted no part of it.

Bob Gunnar had asked her for several files that were usually for Harry's eyes only, and she'd given them to him, not mentioning that Harry expected to be back in the near future. Then she'd settled down to monitoring the radio to see how Sturdley's plan played out.

So far, it definitely had its ups and downs.

"A group of angry giants is walking the streets of Manhattan today," a reporter was saying against a background of blaring sirens. "They're not protesting, but they are using their considerable powers to make life very difficult for criminals. The streets are ringing with sirens as the police go to pick up alleged perpetrators collared by the Fantasy Factory's Heroes. In the space of one block, I saw a giant nab a burglar strolling off with a bag of loot, disarm someone carrying a hidden knife, and scare off a group of street drug-sellers. Pretty impressive, Jim."

The announcer on the all-news station had other information, however. "We're getting reports of backed-up traffic throughout the borough of Manhattan," he said, "and some true horror stories from the subways. With their usual haunts too hot for them right now, thanks to the heroes' intervention, many criminals are apparently heading underground, trying to avoid the long—or in this case, large—arm of the law. What this will mean for rush hour, we do not know."

The operations center of the New York City Transit Police was bedlam. Phones rang, radios blared, and there was a constant high-pitched babble of dispatchers trying to move a limited force of on-duty officers to dozens of trouble scenes all over Manhattan.

Sean O'Banion, the officer in charge, shook his head. This wasn't a crime wave, it was more like a tsunami.

"I got a shot-and-stab at Borough Hall Station," one of the dispatchers said.

That got a double-take from O'Banion. "Usually we get a shooting *or* a stabbing," he said. "Which is this?"

"Both," the dispatcher responded. "Two guys tried to mug each other. One got shot, the other got stabbed."

"Good," O'Banion muttered. "I wish more of them would cancel each other out."

He bit off his words as a lieutenant came in, his hat brimming with gold braids. "The media is parked in Public Affairs asking about an upsurge in crime reports. We've got to up our response time."

"What we've got to do is get more officers on the line," O'Banion said tersely. "Our people are stretched too thin. It's like spitting on a blast furnace."

"More people means overtime, and you know how limited our budget is."

"Then maybe we should just tell the straphangers to *walk* home. They'd be safer."

"Have you tried to get help from the NYPD?" the lieutenant asked.

"They're busy enough in the streets, collaring guys busted by the Heroes—giants—whatever you want to call them. I think it's a shame they don't fit down in the subways." O'Banion shook his head. "Any scuzzball with brains in this city is heading underground. You might say we've got the cream of the scum of five boroughs riding the rails tonight."

"Don't you have any suggestions on how to stop them?"

O'Banion gave his boss a grim smile. "Have you considered flooding the tunnels?"

Rafe and Georgie eyed the traffic heading down the main road to the bridge, then glanced to see what was coming along the side street. This had been a good corner for them, for their "firm" as they called it, and their scam "bump and run."

They'd gotten their parts down perfectly. Skinny, agile Rafe landed on the hood of a passing car coming down the side street. Sometimes he was good enough to convince his partner Georgie that he'd really been hit. When the driver stopped the car, it was Georgie's turn to play. With his tree trunk-like arms, he'd either grab the driver as she (usually they went for women) came out of the car to check on Rafe's condition, or if they stopped but didn't oblige by exiting, it was Georgie's job to drag them out. The boys wound up with a free car and usually the victim's bag, with money, credit cards, and keys.

"Ooh," Rafe said, his whole body vibrating. "Here comes a good one."

It was a late-model convertible, out of place in the neighborhood, driven by a young, pretty blond girl who looked obviously lost. A suburban teen queen, just passing through the city, Georgie thought. He'd enjoy yanking on her.

Rafe was getting ready to dart between two parked cars and do his acrobatic act when the bridge traffic suddenly seemed to stop altogether. Horns sounded, people on the street were turning . . . and a shadow fell over them.

The guys looked up to see an eighteen-foot-tall woman in a white costume and bright red hair looking at them the way cats look at mice. "You can try it, but you'll never make the bridge. Now why don't you run before I bump *you*?"

A huge foot stomped the ground behind Georgie with great authority. Rafe was already across the street, and Georgie was heading in a different direction. For today, at least, their firm was dissolved.

* * *

By the time the uptown local reached 110th Street, Deke Trevis was a deeply disappointed man. He'd lifted three different wallets in three different cars of the train, and each time been relieved of them, once by a guy with a knife, once by a guy with a sharpened screwdriver, and once by a wacked-out crazy with a gun.

I thought working the trains instead of the streets today would keep me out of trouble, he thought sourly.

He should have gotten off at 116th Street. Instead, he'd only moved to the first car, trying to stay away from all the action. But now the gunman had made his way up there, collecting forced donations from everybody he passed.

Sweat trickled down Deke's sides as he watched the guy come swaggering toward him. He was suddenly silhouetted by a burst of light from ahead of the train. Deke remembered that this line ran on a stretch of elevated track between 125th and 137th Streets.

He glanced out the front window of the car—and saw a giant arm stretched across the tracks.

The motorman saw it, too, jerking the car to a screeching halt.

"What the—" the gunman said as he was thrown to his knees.

Then the side window of the car was smashed in by an oversized fist, a fist that reached inside to engulf the gunman's weapon.

In seconds, the man was disarmed and dragged screaming out the shattered window.

Deke slunk low in his chair, but a moment later the hand was back.

"You have no secrets from me, Deke Trevis."

* * *

"Peg. Peg."

Peg Faber slowly realized that someone was standing in front of her desk, and from the tone of voice, had been trying for some time to get her attention.

She looked up and saw John Cameron leaning over her, concern in his eyes.

"Sorry, John," she said, embarrassed. "I guess I just wasn't with it."

"No need to apologize," John replied. "I'm famous for zoning out around here."

"What can I do for you?"

"I thought . . . He cleared his voice nervously. "Maybe we could grab a late lunch."

Peg looked at her watch and realized that there was an empty as well as a sinking sensation in her stomach. "I don't know—" she began.

Then she heard the sound of raised voices from behind Bob Gunnar's door. Peg made up her mind and grabbed her purse. "Yes, I do. Let's get out of here."

The afternoon was sunny and warm, a wonderful contrast to the poisonous atmosphere inside the office. They went to a little sidestreet cafe, where John demolished a burger and fries while Peg picked at an omelet.

Glancing up, they both spoke the same words at the same time: "I'm scared."

Peg gawked for a second, then took a gulp of coffee. "Have you heard anything about what's going on in the city?"

John nodded. "I got the guys in the mail room to tune their boom box to a news station."

Peg twirled a nervous finger around the top of her

cup. "I don't think Harry's plan is getting him what he needs. What's happened on the subway—" She rubbed her arms, even though it was a warm day. "I think we should call it off, before it backfires."

"How can *we* call it off?" John asked. "It's Mr. Sturdley's plan."

"Maybe you should talk to Robert," Peg suggested.

John quickly shook his head. "Not him," he said. "Besides, the giants are spread out all over the place. We have no way to call them in." His eyes looked haunted. "That's what worries me. They're on their own, unsupervised—"

"What's it to you?" Peg suddenly flared. "If you don't like things, you can just Rift off to your pocket universe. Or take a brief vacation someplace, like you did before."

She stopped at the expression on his face, the sudden hurt in his eyes.

"I—that didn't come out the way I wanted. I'm sorry," Peg said.

"No, you're right. But Peg, I don't have tights and a cape. I don't know what to do." John's big hands were bunched into fists as he stared down at his plate.

"I tried to warn you. Real life doesn't work like comic books." Peg reached out to touch one of John's hands. He pulled away, raising oddly pale eyes to look at her.

"Y'know," John said quietly, "maybe we were better off the way we started, with you the prettiest girl in the Fantasy Factory and me the office geek."

"Just about the only girl in the office," she said with a weak smile.

"Yeah, with Zeb Grantfield drawing you into his books."

"You used to surprise me sometimes," Peg admitted, "taking care of things I needed before I even knew I needed them done." She paused. "I wish I understood you, John Cameron."

"That makes two of us," John said. "It's all so new to me." He shook his head. "It's a lot easier when people just think you're a goofball."

"But a lovable goofball," Peg said.

John's face brightened for a moment, and he smiled. "Maybe we can go and see Mr. McManus. He might be able to help."

The waiter brought their bill, which Peg intercepted before John could get to it. "Don't be stupid. I know they haven't cut you a check yet for *Robert*."

"That's the problem with you, Peg. You know everything, and want to know more."

They were halfway down the block when a red sports car came screaming through a turn off Madison Avenue, hopping the curb and barreling straight for them. John seized hold of Peg and spun her into the doorway of a little bookstore, his arms wrapped tightly around her.

The convertible careened past, and a second later they heard the jolting footsteps of a hero pounding in hot pursuit.

John and Peg, arms still around each other, peered out from their safe haven. The sidestreet was pretty much empty, but the end was jammed with gridlocked traffic on the avenue. The intersection was wall-to-wall vehicles. The sports car couldn't push its way in. The pursuing giant caught up, reached down, and yanked the driver from behind the wheel.

"That car doesn't belong to you, does it?" the hero boomed in an angry voice. They recognized him now as Thomas, the sandy-haired giant whom Harry had described as having Murphy Anderson abdominals. Sturdley considered him photogenic enough for his own book—*The Terrific Thomas*.

"I don't like thieves," Thomas growled.

"Look, man! It isn't like I love doing this. I got to make a living," the car thief babbled as he dangled from the giant's hands.

Thomas gave him a piercing gaze. "Oh, you're just the fall guy, is that it? Well, little man, you should watch out for falls."

The giant held the thief around the torso, then tossed him a good thirty feet into the air.

High-pitched screams erupted from the thief as he dropped, was caught by Thomas, then thrown into the air again.

Peg turned away as the sadistic game of catch continued. "So much for Pantagruel," she said.

"Pantagruel? Is that a new comic I haven't seen yet?" John asked.

She looked at him and laughed. "Rabelais, John. His giants weren't just figures of fun. They stood for a philosophy: largeness of soul."

Thomas laughed as he tossed his captive again.

Peg shook her head. "Our giants are just *large*."

Finally bored, Thomas dumped the quivering thief. The man was deathly pale, his eyes large and glassy. But as soon as he hit the sidewalk, be began scrabbling in the direction of the IRT station.

All amusement dropped from Thomas' face. "No, little man! You're not going in there. You're not getting away."

He seized the thief's shirt and struck him, open-handed. After three blows, the man hung like a doll in the giant's hand. Blood trickled from the thief's nose, mouth, and one ear.

Peg screamed and burrowed into John's arms.

Thomas turned toward them, sneered, then stopped, a look of recognition dawning on his face. Leaving the senseless thief, the giant headed toward them.

CHAPTER 20

"It's New York's *First Person News*—the Eleven O'clock Report." The announcer's voice came over a trumpet fanfare that segued into newsroom noise.

"We are now eight hours into Operation Hero, and to say the least, New York has never seen a day like this."

Video footage showed a wizened old grandmotherly type walking in a public park. She held out a battered old leather handbag with a tarnished brass clasp. "I've been afraid to take this out with me for ten years," she said, leaning heavily on her walker. "But today, I can take all my things with me and sit out here enjoying the flowers."

In the background could be seen the enormous shape of a white-costumed hero passing by.

"That's one view of this afternoon's experiment in crime-fighting," the newscaster said. "But here's another."

A quick cut showed an almost hysterical young woman coming up out of the subway. Her clothes were ripped, her cheek was swollen and, as her head shook, Harry Sturdley could see that her earlobe was bleeding where someone must have torn loose an earring.

"They're like animals down there—animals!" she cried, tears running down her face.

An annoyed young man, looking like he'd just emerged from a combat zone, stepped in front of the camera. "Can't you leave her alone?" he shouted.

"Can you tell us what's going on aboard the trains?" a reporter asked.

"It's hell down there," the man said briefly. "Now get out of my way. I gotta find a bus and get home."

Harry ran a hand over his eyes. "What have I done?" he whispered to himself. "What have I done?"

He hadn't even thought of the subway system when he'd so blithely issued his orders to the giants. Instead of ending crime, he'd just driven the underworld underground.

The plastic chair wobbled under Harry as he shifted around in it. Government issue—the INS downtown detention center was hardly built for comfort, although his accommodations were probably the top of the line. Harry, receiving VIP treatment thanks to all the media attention, had a private cell on the fourth floor, and no company. He was now in the prisoner's deserted lounge, wondering where the other prisoners could be as he watched the TV news.

I never thought I'd ever listen to John Cameron, Sturdley thought, *but maybe the kid was right.*

Leslie Ann Nasotrudere appeared on the screen with tape of some new giant atrocity. Harry turned down the sound and stepped over to the lounge window. It could be opened, a surprise in a Wall Street building, but beyond the glass was steel mesh.

He had a surprisingly good view of the Hudson River, only a block or so away. Harry's idle gaze suddenly sharpened. There was a figure in the water—out of scale and swimming his way. He stared in disbelief as a giant climbed out of the Hudson, then dashed swiftly and silently right for the INS building . . . and Harry.

The Hero wore his white uniform pants, now sagging with water, and nothing else. Using fingers and toes, he began scaling the high-rise, aiming for the window where Sturdley stood.

Harry leaned forward as giant fingers hooked themselves in the wire mesh and pulled the giant's face into view.

It wasn't Robert. This was a giant named Gideon, half a head shorter than even Maurice, who was on the small side for a giant. Gideon also lacked the usual Hero's physique, being more stringy than muscular.

Sturdley had noticed him in the group of giant expatriates because he was against type. Gideon had been limping, and he'd been more severely bruised and battered than the others.

Robert had never discussed the struggle that had taken place as the giants left their homeworld, but he had mentioned that Gideon was the last to join them.

The giant's raw-boned face was creased with worry as well as the strain of his climb.

"Robert shouldn't have sent you," Harry said in a low voice. "If the guards—"

"I don't care about your human guards." Gideon's voice was a hoarse whisper. "It's Robert and the others

I'm afraid of. That's why I snuck away to speak with you here."

"About what?" Sturdley was completely confused.

"Listen, you've got to get a message to Robert—"

"No, *you* listen. I had hoped that things might be different when we came here, that the others might have learned something from the chaos that engulfed them. But they don't care. I saw the way they were treating your people on the street today. They won't listen. They'll turn your world into what mine became. That's why I have to warn you—"

His voice broke off in a choked cry as his face suddenly disappeared. Harry leaned forward, pressing his face against the metal mesh, to see what had happened.

Gideon had been yanked from the wall by another pair of giant hands or rather, by several pairs. Harry made out at least three other Heroes in the shadows at the base of the building. They all pounced on the tumbling Gideon.

The fight was short and vicious, all the more chilling because it took place in silence. A hand clapped over Gideon's mouth as soon as he fell among the giants waiting below. Each of the ambushers alone was bigger and heavier than the little giant. Nonetheless, Gideon nearly tore his way free, jabbing with elbows and knees.

Then a brutal fist smashed into the side of his head. Gideon was overcome after that, but the attackers continued to work him over, still taking care to smother his cries.

It was a bizarre montage; one moment violent action,

the next stillness. The three figures—Harry never saw their faces—abruptly bundled off Gideon.

"Harry," a voice whispered. Then Robert was climbing up to Harry's window. "That was close!"

"What—what's going on?" Sturdley demanded.

"We've just saved your life," Robert told him. His lips curved in a mirthless grin. "Gideon . . . was not one of us. He lived alone in the woods, had strange ideas. If I had known how strange, I would never have brought him here. The man was mad, Harry, raving mad. He had conceived some insane grudge against you."

"You mean, he came here to—" Sturdley couldn't finish. "But he said he had to give me a warning."

He tried to peer past the head that took up most of the window. Gideon and his three captors were back at the river. The three Heroes entered the water, dragging the limp form along with them.

Belated recognition sent a chill through Harry. Robert had just referred to Gideon in the past tense, as if he were dead.

The blond giant moved to fill Harry's field of vision. "That was just a ploy to let him get close to you. You have enough troubles right now without having a murderer after you."

Sturdley jammed shaking hands into his pockets. "Look, about Operation Hero—"

Robert shook his head. "Not as effective as we might have hoped, but we've been learning. We've broken into teams now, some to chase the criminals, others to guard the ratholes they would dart into. Your police have sent more guards into the subways. It may take longer than you thought, but we will win."

The sculptured face took on a faraway look. "We *will* win."

Robert suddenly focused again on Harry. "Rest assured, we'll be doing our best for you." The giant smiled. "After all, aren't we your Heroes?"

Robert disappeared from the window, and Harry staggered back to his chair, moving like an old man, the vision of Robert's huge, solidly muscled body in a skintight unitard burned into his brain. "The tighter the uniform," he muttered to himself, "the stranger the hero."

*Superheroes, deadly games,
assassination attempts and
a strange odyssey through the rift
are all in HEROES WORLD,
coming in February, 1994.*

STAN LEE, the publisher of Marvel Comics and creative head of Marvel Entertainment, is known to millions as the man whose superheroes propelled Marvel to its prominent position in the comic book industry. Hundreds of legendary characters, such as Spider-Man, The Incredible Hulk, The Fantastic Four, Iron Man, Daredevil, and Dr. Strange all grew out of his fertile imagination. Stan has written more than a dozen best-selling books for Simon & Schuster, Harper & Row and other major publishers. Most recently, he wrote the introduction to *Marvel: Five Fabulous Decades of the World's Greatest Comics*, which details the growth of Marvel and Stan's career. When Marvel made the decision to launch an animation studio on the west coast, Stan moved to Los Angeles to become creative head of Marvel's new cinematic venture, Marvel Productions Ltd.

WILLIAM McCAY has written over thirty novels for the juvenile, young adult, and adult markets. His most recent book, the Star Trek novel *Chains of Command*, was on the *New York Times'* Paperback Bestseller list for three weeks. At the same time, Mr. McCay had four titles on the Waldenbooks juvenile bestseller list—each from the Young Indiana Jones series, which he launched for Random House with *The Plantation Treasure* in 1990. A fifth Indiana Jones novel, *The Secret Peace*, came out in May 1992. He has also written a number of single titles, including a horror story, a crime novel, and a non-fiction work of speculative science.

DAVE GIBBONS has been a professional cartoonist since 1973, contributing frequently to *2000 A.D.*, illustrating "Harlem Heroes," "Dan Dare," and "Rogue Trooper." Since then, he has drawn and written for most comics publishers on both sides of the Atlantic. His work has encompassed "Dr. Who," "Superman," "Batman," "Green Lantern," the Hugo award-winning *Watchmen*, and *Give Me Liberty*.

Your feedback on Riftworld is important to us. We welcome all of your questions about the series, including your reactions to the Fantasy Factory comics characters. Letters can be sent to:

Byron Preiss Visual Publications, Inc.
Attn: Stan Lee's Riftworld
24 W. 25th Street
New York, NY 10010

If you and/or a friend would like to receive the *ROC Advance*, a bimonthly newsletter featuring all the newest and hottest ROC books and authors, on a complimentary basis, please fill out this form and return it to:

ROC Books/Penguin USA
375 Hudson Street
New York, NY 10014

Your Address
Name _____
Street _____ Apt. # _____
City _____ State _____ Zip _____

Friend's Address
Name _____
Street _____ Apt. # _____
City _____ State _____ Zip _____